ROBIN HOOD

A BANCROFT

CLASSIC

BANCROFT BOOKS
LONDON

BANCROFT BOOKS
49–50 Poland Street
London W.1

First published in the "Bancroft Classics" 1968
This impression 1972

430 00099 5

CONTENTS

Chapter I

THE ARRIVAL OF ROBIN HOOD

A SHAFT of moonlight glinted down through the heavily leafed branches of the trees, and caught the side of a solidly built but very small chapel.

There was not a movement in the forest, and it looked as though every living thing was holding its breath seemingly waiting for something to happen. Then suddenly the tall figure of a man stepped from amongst the trees, and moved towards the chapel, glancing anxiously about him as he did so, and then he hurried up the rough stone steps and unlocked the door with the aid of a heavy key that he carried on a string attached to his leather belt. He pushed open the heavy oak door and hastened inside, closing the door gently behind him.

He strode up the aisle and a few moments later, just as he had completed the lighting of the altar candles, he heard a gentle tapping on the door, a tapping that was obviously in a pre-arranged rhythm. Tap tap, tap tap, tap tap.

He opened the door a few inches and peered out at the callers, and then admitted them with a welcoming smile lighting up his dour face, and then carefully locked the door behind them.

While they were taking off their long black cloaks, he slipped off his own cloak and knelt down in his priests robes before the altar to pray, and after this, he turned to greet the couple as they moved slowly up the aisle hand in hand.

"You must hurry," whispered the young man urgently, "for I feel that we have been followed, and I am determined to marry Joanna before we are caught, and she dragged back to the castle by her father."

"Is he still dead against this marriage," asked the priest sadly.

"Yes," said the bride, "just because William Fitzooth is half Saxon and half Norman, my father has forbidden me ever to see my love again. The Normans did great wrong to him, and now he hates every drop of Norman blood, unreasonably at times."

"I know that Sir George Gamwell of Gamwell Hall suffered greatly at the hands of the Normans," said the priest quietly, "but as you are obviously so much in love with each other, I will perform the ceremony, and I pray that your life together may be long and happy, and that you will have many children to bless you."

So saying, the priest opened his prayer book and began the marriage service, and soon afterwards, the newly married couple slipped quietly away into the forest to mount their waiting horses and ride along the narrow path to the home of William Fitzooth, the great house called Locksley Hall.

Sir George was, at the time of the marriage, busily preparing for a trip overseas, and just as he was about to go and say farewell to his daughter, a messenger from Prince John rode up to the hall on such urgent business, that Sir George forgot all else but the business in hand and rode off into the night with his followers at his heels and the Prince's messenger riding like the wind a few yards ahead of him.

Therefore it was almost a year before he returned home and learned of his daughter's elopement, so carefully had the secret been kept by the servants who loved her far more than they loved her surly father. When he heard the news, he sank down on to a chair in the great hall overcome for the moment, and speechless with rage.

When he could speak again, he roared, "How dare they marry against my wishes? How dare they? But I will put an end to this madness straight away, I will not have Norman blood in my family. I above all people, after all that the Normans have done to me. Saddle my horse immediately, and order my six best swordsmen to accompany me on a mission. Immediately! What are you waiting for? Get moving and do as I say. I will not let my daughter remain in that man's house one moment longer than I can help."

The servants ran to do his bidding, and the horses were saddled in record time, and were soon fretting at the main entrance, waiting for Lord Fitzwalter and his six fighting men to mount them.

Lord Fitzwalter rushed down the steps of Gamwell Hall with his men at his heels, and he shouted instructions to them in a voice that could be heard all the way across the smooth green lawns and park lands to the very edge of Sherwood Forest. The birds in the massive oak trees took flight at the noise, and flew in terror into the woods out of harm's way. Then the horses were being whipped brutally by the infuriated nobleman and his soldiers, as they gathered speed on their journey to the home of William Fitzooth and his wife.

By the time the journey had been completed, the horses were wet with sweat and covered in flecks of white foam, and they were breathing hard through their nostrils.

William Fitzooth was just returning from a short hunting expedition in the forest when he saw the horsemen riding madly up the road in the direction of his house, and he paused for a moment to watch them anxiously, wondering what bad news they could possibly be bringing him. In the very troubled state that England was in at the moment, anything was possible, and he watched anxiously as the men descended from their horses and hurried up the steps to confront him angrily.

His hand went automatically to his sword, as he saw their angry faces, but he did not draw his weapon.

He rode after them to the entrance of his house, and when he was within speaking distance, he shouted, "What is the trouble? Why the haste? What is wrong?"

"Trouble," roared Sir George, "what is the trouble? You should know that without having to ask, you villain. Where is my daughter? Bring her to me at once and saddle a horse for her. Immediately, I say! Immediately!"

Sir George almost shrieked the words, and it was only at this moment that William recognised his angry caller and saw that he was speaking to his own father-in-law, Sir George Gamwell. Sir George whipped off the hat that he was wearing, and pushed his fair saxon hair out of his eyes.

Words seemed to fail him for a few moments and he choked. When he had recovered himself a little, he shouted, "Bring my daughter to me. Get her a horse. She is to ride home with me immediately."

"My wife Joanna is not well enough to ride anywhere at this moment," cried William firmly, "for at any moment now, a child will be born to bless our marriage. But come inside, Sir George. I will order my servants to serve you with something cooling to drink. You and your men."

Sir George followed William into the house without a word, and glanced about the great hall as he moved into welcome shade and coolness. He sank down on to a comfortable chair, and moments later, was drinking a flagon of fresh milk, and his men who were now sitting on the steps outside, were also enjoying the refreshing drink.

Sir George felt his temper cool suddenly when William had mentioned the expected child, and now his thoughts were on his daughter, and his feelings of rage were replaced by feelings of anxiety. William was pacing up and down the floor, his forehead creased into worried lines, and he chewed his knuckles as he waited news from the doctor who was upstairs with Lady Joanna.

"I have grown to love Joanna more and more deeply as the days have gone by," said William gently, "and she loves me more and more. We are very happy together, Sir George. This child will almost set the seal on our happiness. Almost but not quite, for it is a great sorrow to us both that you did not approve of our marriage. If you could forgive and forget my Norman blood, and just regard me as an ordinary man who loves his wife and his family, our cup of happiness would be overflowing with everything good."

Sir George drew a deep breath as though to speak, but the words were never uttered, for suddenly through the silent house, came the sound of the lusty cry of a newly born baby. William gave a great cry of joy, and Sir George rose to his feet, feeling a great sweep of relief washing over him.

"My grand-child," he said, his voice breaking with emotion, "my very own first grand-child. My daughter's child."

William ran up the stairs two at a time, and disappeared from view.

He did not return for quite a while, and Sir George was left alone to think matters out more calmly as he paced up and down the spotlessly clean floor of the great hall, thinking that perhaps he had been too hasty and too bigotted when he forbade the marriage. William had the appearance of a very happy man, and the house was beautifully furnished and the gardens were perfection. The atmosphere of the great house was that of a home, a real home where contented people dwelt. On the great oak table in the hall lay a childs toy, obviously waiting to be given to its new owner. Sir George picked up the tiny bow and arrow, and fingered it gently, a smile breaking through on his face. If he went against Joanna now, he would be cutting himself off from contact with his daughter and his grand-child, and even his feelings against the Normans could not justify him from cutting off all the joy and happiness that would otherwise be his.

"What will William and Joanna do if the child is a girl," he said quietly.

Then he whirled round and looked up expectantly at William, who was walking down the stairs with something in his arms. That something was a baby wrapped in snow white wrappings. William walked gently down the stairs and across the great hall towards the new grandfather.

William smiled proudly, and said, "Allow me to present to you my new son. This is Robert, but we shall call him Robin."

Sir George took hold of the baby's fingers, and tears came in to his eyes as he beheld the child.

"Robin," he said, moving the hood that rested on the child's head, "Robin Hood. I will certainly forgive you both. In fact, I beg your forgiveness. Now let us go and see Joanna, I have got to see her as quickly as possible. I have not seen her for some months, and we have much to talk about. Please let me carry the child."

So saying, Sir George took Robin in his arms and walked up the stairs to his daughter's bed-chamber, whilst William followed him glowing with happiness and carryng the tiny bow and arrow in his powerful hands.

Chapter II

ROBIN FITZOOTH

WHEN Richard the First, known as Richard the Lion Heart, came to the throne of England in 1189, his mind was far away from matters of state, for he was a soldier born and bred. After a year of what he considered to be the dullest time of his life, ruling and attending to all the routine matters that a King had to deal with in those days, he became unbearably restless and pulled up his roots to go out to Palestine to fight a Holy War against Saladin. He left the ruling of England to the Bishop of Ely, a trusted friend, and lost himself in the fighting of a war that took all his thoughts and energies away from England and what was going on there.

Prince John rubbed his hands with glee when he bade Richard farewell and watched the ship sail away, for he knew very well that if Richard lost his life in the wars or died a natural death from some foreign disease, he was next in succession to the throne of England, and he dreamed of the day when he would be King John.

The Bishop of Ely was a good man, but quite useless when it came to dealing with unscrupulous men who wished Richard nothing but harm, and it was not long before this worthy man of the Church had to fly for his life, with John's men on his tail.

After this came a reign of terror in England, as John set to work taxing the people of every coin that he could squeeze out of them, and he showed only too clearly that he cared for money and power above everything else, and fair dealing was looked upon by him as mere softness. He outlawed the gentry for imagined crimes and seized their properties and money, and many of them fled out of sheer desperation to Palestine to fight with Richard just to get out of the clutches of the wicked prince.

John set up Sheriffs over counties, and used them purely and simply as tax gatherers and doers of all his dirty work in their regions. The Sheriff of Nottingham was the worst Sheriff of the lot, and he soon became hated and feared by everybody who came in contact with him, and most people did come in to contact with him in the most painful of ways.

It was under these conditions that Robin Fitzooth grew to manhood, and he learned early in life to despise the Sheriff and his way of going on. Robin helped the poor as much as he could, but there was nothing much that he could do in the face of the wide scale activities of the Sheriff and Prince John. He would have needed a mint full of money, to help to undo all the harm that the greed of the Prince was bringing about.

One day as Robin was walking through Nottingham on a matter of business, he saw a strange procession coming towards him. A hand full of the Sheriff's men were riding along on their sprightly horses, dragging a rope behind them, and attached to the end of the rope was a poor forester that Robin knew well.

"Help me!" shouted the man as he was dragged past Robin. "They are going to hang me because I cannot pay the taxes they demand. Help me, please."

Robin pushed his way through the crowds, uttering words of instruction to the people as he did so. When he reached the man, he drew a knife and cut the rope.

"Get lost amongst the crowd," whispered Robin, "and then go up that side street. Come to my house if you find that you need any further help."

The crowd clustered round the horsemen and made progress so difficult for them, that the soldiers did not notice until they reached the forest, that the man they were now dragging along behind them, was none other than one of the Sheriff's most ardent supporters. Robin had tied the rope round the man in the middle of the mob, unseen and un-noticed, and the real prisoner had escaped into the cluttered up narrow streets of the ancient little town.

"When the Sheriff hears of this," cried the Captain, "he will have us hanged."

He untied the man and begged his forgiveness most abjectly for this happening, but the man was as embarrassed as the Captain, and asked him to say no more about it.

"If the news gets out that I was tied up in place of the prisoner who was obviously rescued by somebody or other, I shall be laughed out of town," said the man, "but if ever I find out who played the trick on me, I shall have my revenge."

"I saw Robin Fitzooth in the crowd at one time," put in one of the soldiers, "and he was there at the time when we were jostled so badly that our horses reared and nearly threw us. He has no love for the Sheriff, and does all kinds of tricks to make things difficult for him."

"Robin Fitzooth," cried the man excitedly, "he has played right into my hands. Tonight he is to be married, or so he thinks. I have an idea, just leave everything to me. I'll have my revenge. Give me a lift back in to town on the back of your horse, good Captain, there is not a moment to be lost. Your men can dig a false grave and fill it with stones, in case the Sheriff wants to see the grave for some reason or other."

"But that will mean that the forester will get away and there will be no search for him," said the Captain.

"That would be better than you and your men being hanged for incompetence," replied the victim of the jape, "back to Nottingham as fast as you can, you can put me down outside the city walls."

An hour later, the Sheriff received a visitor, a certain Jeremy Cramp.

"What can I do for you," asked the Sheriff curtly, looking up from the table where he was working his way through a mass of papers and lists and money boxes. "Be brief, as I have much work to do."

"I have information that you may be able to make use of," smirked Master Cramp, the victim of Robin's little joke earlier in the day, "I believe that you know a certain Robin Fitzooth, the self styled Earl of Huntingdon."

"Self styled is the correct way to put it," snapped the Sheriff, "he claims that he is the Earl by right of his mother and the Saxon line of the Earl his father. He is no friend of mine, he is obsessed with King Richard. What news of him have you got?"

Jeremy Cramp smirked at the Sheriff as he said, "Tonight he is to be married to Lady Marion, daughter of Lord Fitzwalter. A great feast is to be held at Locklesley Hall before the even. I thought that you might wish to ... er ... attend as ... shall we say, un-invited guests. You and some of your soldiers, if you see what I mean."

"Why should I wish to attend," snarled the Sheriff.

"You might like to ... er ... repay a debt or two," whispered Jeremy Cramp, "you must owe the Earl quite a few grudges by now, for he always seems to be working against you. I too, would like to see this upstart who calls himself an Earl, brought down a peg or two."

The Sheriff looked at the man coldly, and snapped, "Away with you! Do not come here nattering to me with your silly ideas. I have more to do than play jokes on Robin Fitzooth. Thank you for paying me a visit, but I have no more time to spare. Good day to you, Master Cramp. By the way, you owe me a hundred gold coins in taxation for a small matter of a deal you did a day or two ago."

Cramp stared at the Sheriff in astonishment and gasped out, "But I owe you nothing. I have had no business deals this week."

"If you will pay me now," said the Sheriff, reaching out a hand that looked like a greedy claw across the table, "I might give further consideration to the little matter that you have just mentioned. One hundred golden coins, please, Master Cramp. Then maybe I will go along to the wedding. But if you say one word about this matter to anybody else, I will have five hundred coins from you, and that fine house of yours also. I am in need of a country house where I can rest at the week-ends. Nottingham gets too hot in the summer months, and the smell of the peasants makes me sick."

Jeremy Cramp pulled a purse out of his pocket, and counted out the hundred golden coins, leaving himself with merely twenty five coins.

"Did I say one hundred coins," smiled the Sheriff, his eyes bright with greed, "I really meant one hundred and twenty five coins."

Cramp almost threw the purse at the Sheriff, but curbed his temper when he saw the glint in the other man's eyes. He poured the rest of the money into the Sheriff's cupped hands, and then bowed his way out of the room, the empty purse dangling from his fingers.

The Sheriff smiled thinly to himself, glanced around to make sure that he was alone, and then he put the money into his own purse.

"Nobody will ever hear of this little transaction," he muttered to himself. "I fancy that Master Cramp paid me so readily, because he too has a score to settle, but he has not got the guts to do the job for himself."

That evening, the Sheriff put on a simple garb and threw a dark cloak around his shoulders, and accompanied by four servants who carried daggers under their tunics, made his way to Locksley Hall, bearing a large package that contained the customary wedding present. It was a painting of Nottingham Castle, painted by the Sheriff himself in one of his rare leisure moments.

The small party joined the throng that were making their way to Locksley Hall, the home of the Fitzooth family, and managed to slip unnoticed into the house. The Sheriff handed over the wedding present, and then made his way to the banquetting hall, and squeezed himself on to one of the already over crowded benches.

The bride and groom made a handsome couple as they walked in to the hall and made their way to the head of the table. Robin was now thirty years of age, and Marion was twenty five. They made their speeches of welcome, and then sat down to enjoy the fabulous meal that was served to them.

"Robin," whispered Will Scarlet when the feasting was done, and the couple were getting ready to leave for the wedding at Fountains Abbey, "I have reason to belive that the Sheriff of Nottingham is amongst the guests. I saw a painting amongst the wedding gifts a few minutes ago, and it was a painting of Nottingham Castle. I saw the Sheriff himself painting it a long while ago, and since then it has hung in his own private office. I was suspicious as soon as I saw the painting, and a moment ago, I thought that I saw the Sheriff himself amongst the guests. He means mischief, Robin, so watch out."

The wedding party set out from the house on horse back, followed by the hundreds of guests, also riding gaily decorated horses. The Sheriff and his men found that they were encumbered on all sides by the guests, and could not get in front of the merry throng.

"I am afraid we shall have to steal a march on the guests," Robin said to Marion quietly, "Will has warned me that the Sheriff has gate-crashed the reception and is amongst those behind us at this very moment, no doubt. He will try to stop the ceremony, I'm sure. Therefore we must go on ahead and persuade the priest to perform a small private service that will make us man and wife, and then we can go through the whole thing again for the benefit of the guests who will have arrived at the abbey by then. It will give us a chance to see what the Sheriff is up to as well. Come, let us gallop away, I will tell you more as we go along."

Under cover of darkness, Robin and Marion slipped away from the main party and then spurred their horses on, so that they arrived at the abbey a good hour before the rest of the wedding party.

Quietly and privately in one of the side chapels, the priest made them man and wife, and then they settled down in the vestry to await the arrival of the guests.

When everybody had arrived, and were seated, the state wedding began.

The priest reached the part of the service where he had to ask if anybody had any objection to the wedding of the happy pair, when suddenly a voice rang out from the back of the abbey.

"I object," cried the voice of the Sheriff of Nottingham, "Robin Fitzooth is a traitor. The King decrees that he forfeits his lands and his wealth, and he shall be banished in the name of King Richard."

"Produce your evidence," shouted Robin, turning to face the assembly, "show the document and the King's seal and that of the Bishop of Ely, who has been left to rule the country whilst King Richard is away fighting in the Holy Wars. Produce the document, Sheriff."

"The document is still in the Bishop's hands, but I can show it to you in a few days time," mumbled the Sheriff sheepishly.

"I also object to the marriage," cried another voice, and Guy of Gisborne rose to his feet and began to move up the aisle. "Robin Fitzooth's claim to the earldom is false. The old Saxon earls were deprived and outlawed for refusing to obey their rightful King, William of Normandy, and only the earldoms created by the King have any right in law."

"Very well then," cried Robin, "that settles it. From this moment onwards, Robert Fitzooth, Earl of Huntingdon, ceases to exist. I will from this day forward be known merely as Robin Hood, a nick-name given to me by my grandfather, Sir George Gamwell. I shall live where there is freedom and justice until Richard returns to England, and fair dealing and happiness return once more to this tortured and oppressed land. I shall take my wealth with me, and use it to help those who are downtrodden."

"I shall have your lands and property for the King," shouted the Sheriff angrily.

"King Richard will give it all back to me when he returns from the Holy Wars," cried Robin, "I am content to wait until then, for the return of what is rightly mine."

"Traitor!" screamed Guy of Gisborne, torn with rage.

"Soon you will hear from me," went on Robin, "but you will hear from me in a way that will startle you all, for I shall continue to help the poor and the oppressed, and none shall stop me from doing what I believe to be right. As for stopping the wedding, no man can do that, for Marion and I were married quietly in this very Abbey in yonder side chapel, before you all arrived. Let this second wedding be completed, and then I shall ask Marion if she will come and live with me where I think fittest at this time."

"I will follow you to the ends of the earth, Robin," said Marion proudly, "and no man or woman shall stop me. Let the service proceed."

The ceremony was completed with dignity, and Robin and his wife moved into the vestry, followed by the closest relations.

"Lord Fitzwalter," said Robin quietly, after the register had been signed, "please take Marion to a retreat in the woods that she knows about already, and I will follow as soon as possible. I have a little business to transact before I join her in about one hours time."

Robin kissed his bride, and watched her ride away into the forest at her fathers side, and then he returned to the abbey to seek out Guy of Gisborne.

The Knight laughed in his face when Robin confronted him, but Robin merely smiled back pleasantly in return.

"If the brave Knight feels that he would benefit from a little exercise," said Robin with mock courtesy, "I shall be pleased to give him a little run for his money."

"Anything you say," snarled Guy, his ugly face twisted into a gargoyle expression, so great was his hatred, "anything you say."

His hand went to his sword, but Robin said calmly, "Not inside the Church, good Knight, not inside the Church, as you well know."

The two men left the abbey side by side, neither trusting the other to walk behind, and then they made their way to a clearing in the woods, where they drew their swords and engaged in a fight that was to be talked about for many a long day in Nottingham. After a bitterly fought combat, Robin finally lashed out with the flat of his sword and sent Guy of Gisborne reeling to the ground where he lay motionless and bleeding from a score of wounds from Robin's sword. Robin himself seemed to be scarcely scratched.

He stood staring down at his enemy for a few moments, and then he wiped his sword on the soft green grass, before replacing the weapon in its scabbard. After this, he turned and mounted the horse that was waiting for him, and rode off in to the forest, followed by Will Scarlet and a few other close friends.

The Sheriff had been watching the fight from the cover of the surrounding trees, biting his nails in extreme anxiety. It was he who minutes later, went to assist Guy to his feet.

Guy looked at him coldly as he said fiercely, "This has been a bad night for both of us, Sheriff. We have both of us made a deadly enemy. From now on, neither you nor I will have the least vestige of peace. Robin will be for ever at our throats. This is indeed a bad night for us both."

The Sheriff, white in the face, nodded his head before turning away with vengeance burning in his eyes. For a while, he looked like a man on the edge of madness.

As he rode away into the forest, he muttered to himself, "I am not the only man who has made an enemy, Robin Hood has made an enemy too, and I can be a very bad enemy, as he will find out before he is so very much older."

Chapter III

THE NEW HERMIT OF COPMANHURST

Friar Michael Tuck bathed his tired feet in the cool waters of the river, and then replaced his sandals, before setting to work on the few small items of food that he had brought with him from the Monastery that same morning. The bread was stale and the meat was tough, but he could not have expected first class food after the furious argument that he had indulged in with the Abbot, an argument that had ended in his being thrown out into the world outside the sturdy but grim walls of what been his only home for the last five years.

Prince John had been almost black in the face with fury when Friar Tuck had refused to kneel and kiss the Prince's feet by way of penance, after he had refused to do a series of very menial tasks for the Prince that Tuck despised with all his heart.

The Abbot had been forced to throw Tuck out of the Monastery, to save his own skin. Prince John would have had the Abbot hanged and all the wealth of the monastery forfeited to the Prince, if he had not showed his favour for John.

Tuck's fat face glowed with anger as he went through the scene in his own mind, and then he relaxed on the river bank as he realised that he was free of all the irksome restrictons of the Monastery, and that he could now go on his own peaceful way.

It was very pleasant here in Sherwood Forest, and he felt capable of dealing with any dangers that might come his way. His trusty stave and its ancestors had served him well, and the great broad sword that he wore concealed beneath his brown habit, was more than a match for any other sword that it might come in contact with. Friar Tuck felt immune from all the evils of the world at this very happy moment.

A rabbit bolted from the cover of the bracken, made towards the water in a great hurry, and then suddenly spun in to the air with an arrow through it's heart. It was dead before it hit the ground.

Friar Tuck pulled in his feet and sat upright, staring about him as he did so.

A rustling amongst the bushes behind him made turn his head uncomfortably quickly, and he found himself looking into the face of the fiercest looking ruffian that he had encountered for many a long month. The man was dressed in a tattered robe of indescribable origin, and he carried a bow in his right hand, a quiver of arrows was slung round his stooped over shoulders. He stared at Friar Tuck in alarm, and then a thin smile broke out on his dirty face, showing two rows of broken and highly discoloured teeth.

"Good morning, good Friar," said the man in a high pitched voice, "I am the Hermit of Copmanhurst, and I am looking for a dead rabbit. Have you seen one anywhere about?"

"Your deceased friend lies over yonder with what I guess is one of your arrows through his framework," said Tuck, "so you are the Hermit of Copmanhurst. Well, well, well."

"I am indeed," smirked the soiled individual, "at your service, good Friar."

"The Hermit of Copmanhurst," mused the Friar, "I thought that I knew all the hermits there were in this part of the world, but you are unknown to me. There used to be such a hermit, and he was a very good friend of mine. But he died, poor fellow, many years ago."

"Ah, that would be my uncle," said the man in mournful tones, "poor Uncle Mendicus. I loved him well. When he died, I took over the business ... the ... er ... hermitage, I mean."

"Indeed," quoth Friar Tuck, raising his eyebrows so high that they almost disappeared for a few moments into his fringe of hair that encircled his head, leaving a bald moon on the centre of his crown. "I was not aware that . . . er . . . Alfred the Hermit . . . had a nephew. To the best of my knowledge, he had no living relatives at all, and he was a close friend of mine."

"Well," gabbled the man, "he was my adopted uncle, in a manner of speaking, and I gave him the name of Mendicus in an affectionate kind of way. Now allow me to collect my rabbit, it is time that I skinned and cleaned it, and put it in my pot, otherwise it will not be ready for my meal tonight."

"I have often wanted to visit his cave again," said Tuck, rising to his feet, "I will accompany you, and spend a few hours remembering past very happy days with my old friend. Lead the way, good Hermit. I will follow with my meagre possessions. Lead on, good friend, lead on."

The Hermit picked up the rabbit and strode away through the woods, with Friar Tuck marching along at his heels.

"I suppose you are a good holy man and observe all the rules," said Tuck, trying to walk behind the man when he could so easily have outpaced him and been there and back twice, in the time that it would have taken the man to get there once.

"I am very holy," said the man.

"Is that rabbit for today's dinner," asked Tuck quietly.

"It is indeed," replied the man, as he pushed through the undergrowth to search for nuts and berries.

"Today's dinner is to be a rabbit," said Tuck, looking at the man with growing suspicion, "meat for today's dinner. Have you forgotten that today is Friday, and that we must none of us eat meat upon that holy day? You ought to know that, friend Hermit."

"Er . . ." babbled the Hermit, "I made a mistake. The rabbit is for to-morrow's meal, I grow absent-minded in my old age."

The man did not appear to be particularly old to Friar Tuck, but he said nothing.

The Hermit seemed reluctant to return to the Hermitage, and it was night fall by the time the two men reached the cave, after loitering about fishing and catching game. By the time the small home had been reached, Friar Tuck was tired and out of patience with the squirming, and he was convinced, lying Hermit, if such he was.

Friar Tuck was a man of great strength and great weight, but he was not over-fond of exercise, and his feet ached with the weight of the great burden that they carried, and he was glad to sit down in front of the Hermit's cave, and leave the other man to prepare supper and serve it.

The meal was served alarmingly quickly, and Tuck found himself staring down at a dirty wooden platter in his hands, a platter that bore a hunk of stale bread, a piece of cracked and dried up cheese, and a horn mug full of brackish water.

"This is poor fare considering the hunting that we have done during the day," said Friar Tuck.

"It is the best that I can do at such short notice," said the Hermit, "the fish is not cleaned or broiled. That would have taken some time. If you would care to wait, I could prepare a better meal . . . for a fee."

"You charge me for food that I have caught myself," roared Tuck, "you will be asking me for a fee for my nights lodgings next. A bed on the hard ground."

"Yes, indeed," replied the Hermit, "for I am a poor man. Understand?"

"No man is poor who can live on forest fare such as we have caught today," said Tuck, "broil me a couple of trout, and be quick about it, Hermit."

The Hermit twisted his face in to a sour grimace, but went about the preparation of the meal whilst Tuck wandered into the cave to have a look at the premises.

The cave was dark and damp and extremely untidy, and a thin starved hound snarled fiercely at him as he stood looking about him, and made as though to attack him.

"Don't worry hound," said Tuck, "I won't touch your miserable sacks and packages, though I am wondering what is in them all. There seems to be a vast quantity of stuff in there with you."

Tuck then wandered down to the river bank and inspected a flat bottomed boat that was moored there. The boat was river-worthy, but it was shabby and in need of repair.

The meal that followed could have been better cooked, but at least the food was fresh, and did not smell of mould. Tuck threw his bread and cheese to the hound, who snatched it and swallowed it hungrily.

Darkness had begun to fall by the time they had cleared up after the meal, and Tuck threw a few more scraps of food to the obviously starving dog, who wagged its tail at him slightly as it looked up expectantly. It snapped and snarled at the Hermit, as thought it would go for his throat if he went any nearer.

"Some day, I'll put an arrow through that miserable beast," muttered the Hermit to himself.

Friar Tuck realised that there was no love lost between the man and his dog.

"I think I'll sleep out of doors tonight," snapped Friar Tuck angrily, "the air is fresher out here, and I like to get my head down amongst the braken."

He bade his unwilling host a curt good night, and then he strode away to a spot fifty yards away from the cave, and settled down amongst the bushes out of sight and sound of the cave and its miserable occupants.

After a while, the Hermit lit a lantern and placed it on the edge of the encampment, and then settled down to wait, armed with a large and very tasty looking pasty that he fetched from inside the cave. He ate greedily, and Tuck felt his mouth water as he saw the succulent food.

Tuck grumbled to himself about the man's meanness, and then settled down to await developments. He was just nodding off to sleep, when he heard the sound of an animal's hoofs coming towards the cave through the wood, and the hound began to bark furiously.

After a short while, he saw two men and a heavily laden pack mule come in to the clearing, and the so called Hermit rose to his feet and hurried to greet them.

He pointed to the place where Friar Tuck was supposed to be sleeping, and the men lowered their voices so that he could not hear what they were saying. They tied the mule to a tree and it began to eat the grass hungrily. The packs contained gold and silver coins, and mugs and platters of silver ware. The men had also obtained from some source or other, a goodly supply of rich foods.

Tuck watched hungrily as the men sat down and spread the feast before them, leaving some broth to heat up in a pot over the fire that was now blazing merrily. The hound howled miserably at the smell of the food. The sight was too much for Friar Tuck, and he rose to his feet and strode towards the midnight feast, knowing now full well, that he was amongst thieves.

"Ah," he said jovially, "just what I was in need of. That pair of small trout barely filled a hole in my back tooth, so I will join you in your meal, good friends."

They glared at his monk's habit, and he knew very well that they would have killed him if he had not been wearing Church man's clothes. They would have killed him for what little he possessed, and that was very little indeed. His handful of coins, a few extra clothes, and the simplest of eating equipment, plus his state and his broad sword. He doubted if they would have wanted his bible and his prayer book, and could imagine them throwing the holy books on to the fire.

He had picked up his stave and put on his sword beneath his robes before he emerged into the open, for he was a firm believer that even a man of God had the right to fight for his life, and he affirmed frequently that he was more use to other people alive than dead. Therefore he had to protect his own skin.

He stooped to pick up a cold leg of lamb and took a few hearty bites from the joint, and then flung the remainder of the snack to the hound who fell upon it ravenously, and then he picked up a flagon of ale from a rock where the men had set it after drawing some ale from a small barrel that they had brought with them.

"Here's good health and a long life to King Richard, may he reign long and gloriously over us all," he cried, and then he drained the flagon, "God bless him."

"King Richard," choked the Hermit, "down with the useless lout. He would rather be abroad pretending to fight for some strange cause or other, than rule over us here in England. We are for Prince John."

"That does it," cried Friar Tuck.

The flagon crashed on to the rocks as he flung it from him in a rage.

"I have no time for Prince John," shouted Friar Tuck, "he sets men to work robbing the poor just to enrich his own coffers, so that he can eat and drink and play games with his courtiers, and generally waste time and money. I guess that all this stuff that you have stored up in the cave, is stolen property, and you will hand it over to him at the first possible moment."

The men sprang to their feet angrily, and their hands went to the hilts of their swords.

"I'll wager that he has promised to pay you well for stealing gold and silver," shouted Tuck, "but I have heard of his tricks before this. He will hang you all as soon as he has got hold of your loot. You are nothing but cheap common thieves."

The men drew their swords and attacked Friar Tuck without a word of warning, and although he tried to beat them off with his stave, they broke his simple weapon after hitting it several times with their swords.

Thinking that he was un-armed, they stood back and laughed in his face. But Friar Tuck whipped out his sword and gave the thieves the biggest beating that they had ever had in their lives. Soon they were running away into the woods, leaving their goods behind them.

"If you come back here," shouted the Friar at their retreating backs, "I will kill you, or worse still, turn you over to Prince John and tell him how you have failed him. Then he will hang you all, slowly and painfully. The hound will tear you to pieces if you return when I am not in the cave, so don't trouble to come back for the gold and the silver."

When he was sure that the men had really gone, he entered the cave where the hound looked up at him gratefully and with wagging tail, licked his hands. Tuck examined the contents of the cave, and found a wealth of coins and golden and silver table ware, and jewels worth a small fortune.

"Robin Fitzooth takes from the rich when he can give to the poor," said Tuck gleefully, "so I shall do likewise. This treasure trove comes from no poor men, so I shall wait until the opportunity arises, and do some good work with it all."

The hound was now completely friendly, and Tuck knew that he would be able to leave the treasure in the dog's care when he wanted to go hunting, or on some other expedition. Nobody would dare to enter the cave, never mind steal anything, whilst the dog was in office there.

"I'll feed you and build up your strength, dog," he said, "until you are as powerful as any dog in the world. A little training will complete the job."

The Friar slept that night across the entrance to the cave, and the following morning, he cleaned out the place and re-arranged the goods in a tidier way than would have been thought possible a few hours before. He fed the animals, and set off to buy oats and fodder for the mule from a farmer a few miles up river.

He returned to find the hound sitting on guard at the cave entrance, and everything was safe and sound inside.

When a further meal had been disposed of, he said, "I shall call the mule Kismet, because it was fate that brought all these good things my way, doubtless all carried at some time or other, on this worthy animal's back. The hound I shall call Hercules because of the strength that I intend him to develop."

That night, Friar-Tuck settled down to a night of sleep that was to be far more peaceful than the broken sleep of the night before. He rested, fully aware that Hercules would guard both the treasure and himself. Nobody would approach without the hound raising the alarm.

As Friar Tuck drifted off into a deep sleep, he thought of the interesting work that lay ahead of him the following day. The work of getting the boat cleaned and in to good order, so that he could run a very profitable ferry service over the river for wayfarers who would pay him a small fee for the job. If any friends of Prince John came along, they could pay double, and would also be treated to a ducking in mid stream.

Indeed it looked as though his new life was going to be both happy and prosperous.

Then a deep slumber descended upon him, and he slept the sleep of the just.

Chapter IV

THE NEW SETTLEMENT

THAT first night in Sherwood Forest was one of extreme worry and anxiety for Robin Hood and his followers, and Marion, who had been put in a small cave to sleep with a heavy guard at the entrance, slept only fitfully and was thankful when the dawn broke and she was able to wash in the stream that trickled down the hill-side.

The whole party broke their fast on cold meats and bread and water, as the smell of cooking would have guided any soldiers who might have been looking for them, straight to their hiding place.

After the meal, they cleared everything away and covered up their tracks, and then crept silently away deep into the heart of the great forest. Robin Hood and Will Scarlet led the way, Marion followed under a heavy guard, and the remainder of the men walked in duck file along the narrow track that soon vanished altogether, and after this, they had to scramble through the undergrowth.

It was growing dark again before Robin Hood found the place that he was seeking, and then he weaved his way across a piece of solid ground that was almost impossible to discern across a bog that encircled a hill that was covered with trees and great outcrops of rock. The party were almost exhausted by the time they reached safe ground, but Robin urged them on to find caves and clean them out ready for the night, and to make beds of bracken.

"We shall gradually get better equipped as we buy stores and goods," he said, "I have plenty of money hidden away in Nottingham, and we can buy bows and steel tipped arrows from a friend of mine. Cloth for clothing, and other things that we need including bedding and blankets. It will take time, but for the time being, we shall manage."

So Robin Hood and his wife and his merry men slowly got their new home organised, and the encampment became a fortress that the enemy would find hard to take.

Marion fitted in with the life, and grew as brown as a nut from exposure to the hot sun and the open air life that she was now leading, and Robin felt more relaxed and happy than he had felt for many a long day.

The men's time was well filled, what with hunting and fishing and getting the camp organised, but one evening as they were all sitting round the camp fire talking over the days events, Will Scarlet said, "Have you ever heard of the horn of good fortune that is supposed to be hidden in a cave in Sherwood Forest, Robin?"

"I think that everybody has heard the legend," said Robin, "but I do believe that it is far more than a legend, there is more than a little truth in it. But I don't know exactly where it is supposed to lie."

"I know," chipped in Martin Much, a forester who had joined the band shortly after their arrival in the forest, "I can lead you straight to the spot, but I warn you, it is going to be a dangerous job to get it, for it is heavily guarded."

"We shall have to learn to crack all kinds of hard nuts now that we are living with danger," replied Robin, "and I would very much like to try to crack this particular musical nut. The horn would be most useful to me, for summonsing my men when I need extra help or am in danger and need more man power to get me out of trouble that might be on hand at any given moment. Could you lead me to the cave, Martin?"

"I'm sure I could," replied Much, his face glowing with pleasure at the thought of an adventure, for life could become rather dull in the forest with nothing to do but hunt and fish and work, he welcomed the thought of a diversion, "I suggest that we set off as soon as it is night fall, just a handful of us."

Robin chose his men carefully, and left instructions for the guarding of the encampment, and when darkness began to fall, Marion bade him God speed and asked him to be careful and to come back safe and sound.

"I will be waiting for you," she said, "and praying for your safe return."

Much led them through the forest for a good five miles, and then motioned to them to go more slowly and carefully, as they were getting nearer their destination.

Suddenly a snarling sound echoed from amongst the trees, and the men drew their swords and stood waiting for whatever the danger was that was approaching them. The sound echoed from amongst the trees several times, and then all was silent again.

Much beckoned them forward, and they found themselves in front of a cave mouth. Much glanced quickly around him and then he slipped inside the cave. A few moments later, he beckoned to Robin and the other men to follow him inside.

"So far so good," said Much, "but we must go carefully."

At that moment, the great snarl sounded again, but this time it was right behind them, and they realised that they were trapped inside the cave by a great slavering beast that stood in the cave mouth. It was the biggest dog that they ever seen in their lives, and its eyes were as red and glowing as coals on a fire.

"At them, Bane. We want none of Prince John's men here. They are after the magic horn, but they won't get it," cried a rough voice from somewhere above them.

The hound crouched to spring, and then a soft light from above their heads caused Robin to glance quickly upwards, and there he saw a great bearded face staring down at him through a hole in the cave roof, and a massive muscular hand held a blazing torch.

"At them," shouted the man, "what are you waiting for?"

"Bane," said Robin gently, "gently, boy, we won't harm you."

For a few moments the fierce animal stared at them doubtfully, and then flew at them through the gloom as though it would swallow them all at one gulp. The men leaped up on to a high ledge out of its reach for the moment.

"Don't kill it if you can help it," cried Robin, "for that would really turn the owner against us. I will try to tackle the beast."

Robin threw aside his sword, and then jumped down on to the cave floor, seizing the great animal from behind round its shaggy throat. For a few breath-taking minutes, he wrestled with the beast, talking into its ears all the while, and then miraculously, the animal quietened down and crouched snarling at him, in one corner of the cave.

Robin talked quietly to the animal, and soothed it into a state of friendliness. Finally he reached out and touched one of its great shaggy ears. His followers breathed again and relaxed for a few moments. But they were soon on the alert again, for the fierce brute of a man above them, shouted out angrily, "I will not have any dog of mine making friends with John's men. I will kill you all and the dog, before I will allow that."

With a mighty leap, he was down on the cave floor, and wielding a rough club in his right hand, his muscles standing out in great knots on his arms and legs and hands.

"I am no friend of John," cried Robin, "so take it easy, friend. I gather that we are both on the same side. I am for King Richard, God Bless him."

The man held his torch up so that he could see into Robin's face.

"By all the Saints above," he gasped, "it is the Earl of Huntingdon. Your Grace, what are you doing here at midnight in my miserable cave? Tell me."

"I *was* the Earl of Huntingdon," replied Robin, "but there was quite an argument at my wedding, and it caused me to change my way of life entirely. Now I am living in Sherwood Forest with a band of faithful followers, and my wife. I thought that the lucky horn was without an owner, and came to get it for our own use."

"I will strike a bargain with you," said the man, "if you can defeat me in unarmed combat, you will be welcome to the horn. If you can get past Bane to get it then."

"That is a bargain," cried Robin, and he and his followers marched out of the cave and came face to face with one of the most massive men that Robin had ever seen in his life.

A terrific battle followed, and Robin felt several times that he had well and truly met his match. The battle went backwards and forwards, until both men were bathed in sweat and their clothes torn to ribbons. But just as Robin was feeling that he could go on no longer, he felt his opponent suddenly weaken, and Robin threw him to the ground and knelt across the great massive chest, and got a grasp on the man's beard and twisted until the man screamed for mercy, thinking that his head was going to be twisted off his shoulders.

Robin rose to his feet, and the man struggled to his knees, gasping, "You are the winner, Sir Robert, you are the winner. You can have the horn, if Bane will let you have it."

Robin staggered in to the cave, and was nearly knocked to the ground as the great hound put his feet on Robin's shoulders and licked his face. Robin pushed the great hound aside, after patting its shaggy head, and then looked around him for the horn.

Will Scarlet entered the cave behind him, holding up a blazing brand, and Robin saw the famous horn for the very first time. The horn that was to be associated with Robin Hood for ever after.

He climbed up to the ledge where the horn stood, and took it in his hands and gazed at it in wonder for a few moments before raising it to his lips and sounding a blast upon it. The sound was true and clear, and Robin thrilled to its clear note. Then he slung the horn to his belt by its cord, and made his exit from the cave to show the horn to his men. Bane followed at his heels, and the shaggy man looked so woe-begone that Robin said, "Why don't you join us, friend, and then you will not lose the horn but will see it every day of your life, and hear it often too. I want as many fighting men as I can get. What about it, eh?"

"Gladly," said the man, "I will follow Sir Robert to the ends of the earth and back again, nothing will shake me off now. Bane will come with me, won't you, hound?"

Bane gave a mighty bark, and went and sat beside his master.

"Tomorrow morning, Will the Tailor will make you a suit of Lincoln Green," said Robin, "and I shall need a new suit as well."

The journey back to the encampment was undertaken in a far more light-hearted way than the journey in search of the lucky horn, and they were greeted joyfully by those who had stayed behind.

The following day, a feast was put on to celebrate the arrival of the lucky horn into the camp, and after a great meal of roast venison and vegetables and a sweet pasty had been eaten, Robin made a speech to which everybody listened with bated breath. It was a speech that was to be followed to the letter for the rest of their lives together.

"Men," cried Robin Hood, "I stand before you as your leader, and I pray that my dealings with you will always be fair and friendly, and that we shall grow closer and closer together as the years go by. I welcome you all to my band, from the first member who is Will Scarlet, to the newest member who is Rough the Woodsman, who came to us only as recently as last night. We are safe and snug in our little retreat, but I do not intend that we shall lead a life of leisure, for there is much work to be done and it is dangerous work. We must help the poor and the oppressed and those in danger, at the expense of the rich who pass along the Great North Road that passes straight through the forest. It will mean robbing the rich to give to the poor, but I see nothing wrong in that. We are for King Richard and against Prince John and all who do his evil work for him. The Sheriff of Nottingham is now our sworn enemy, and so is Guy of Gisborne, and if any of us fall into either of their hands, we can only expect to be hanged. There is much to be done, and we must range the forest widely, in small and widely spread larger groups, but never alone. That would be asking for trouble. A rescue operation could throw us all into great danger, so take care not to get caught."

The men gave a cheer, but Robin had still more to say.

"I obtained this horn last night after an exciting adventure," he said, "but it is not mine, it belongs to us all. I shall carry it as long as I live, but it will be used for special purposes only. I shall sound it when I need the help of all of you when a job comes along that is too big for myself and the few men that I have with me. I shall also sound it when I am in danger, or one of you is in danger and I want help in rescueing you. It is an alarm call. I will sound it now, so that you will recognise the sound when you hear it."

Robin drew a deep breath and blew a long clear note on the horn.

"The next time that you hear that sound," he said, "you will all come immediately to the spot where the horn is being sounded, for your help will be very urgently needed. Now I would like you all to stand and drink good health and good luck to our enterprises, and then a toast to my beloved wife, Marion of Sherwood Forest."

The toasts were drunk, and then three great cheers rang through the forest.

Robin Hood and his merry men were in residence in the greenwood, and ready to do whatever work came their way, in the best and fairest way possible.

Chapter V

THE TAX GATHERERS

"A FINE LOT OF TREES," said the Sheriff, rubbing his thin and claw-like hands together, "Prince John will be delighted. But of course, you will not expect to receive the price that they will fetch in London, as you already owe far more than that price in taxes. The money will be kept by the Prince's treasury, and you will have to pay the rest of it out of your own pocket. A further tax of two hundred guineas, that is what you owe."

The forester and his wife stared at the Sheriff in dismay, and were silent for a few stricken moments, and then the Sheriff said, "You do understand what I mean, of course. You still owe two hundred guineas in taxation, and you will be required to pay that sum within a week, or there will be serious trouble coming your way. The Prince does not like to be kept waiting for his money."

"But I haven't got two hundred guineas," gasped the forester, "I have barely enough money left to buy food for the week. How can I possibly owe the Prince all that money, anyway?"

"Perhaps I ought to explain," said the Sheriff, "there is a new tree felling tax in force now, each forester will have to pay a small amount of tax on each tree that he fells each year."

"But I already pay the Prince extra rent on this part of the forest," argued the forester, "by the time I have paid the rent and the taxes that I know about, I have scarcely anything left. I am being taxed out of existence."

The Sheriff looked at him coldly and said with a sneer, "If you object to paying the rent and the various taxes, we could easily make a little adjustment. The Prince could take over this part of the forest, and maybe you could find another way of earning your living."

"Take this land away from me," cried the forester, "but he can't do that."

"He has done it to others," said the Sheriff coldly, "and he could easily do it to you."

"I shall have to think the matter over," moaned the forester, "I don't know what to do, I don't know what to think at this moment."

The Sheriff remounted his horse and said, "I will call to see you tomorrow, I must go now as I have various other taxes to collect. More money to get together for our dear Prince John."

He spurred his horse and rode away in to the forest, with twelve soldiers on horseback behind him, to protect him from any enemies that might be lurking amongst the trees.

Before the forester and his wife had time to collect their thoughts, they heard the sound of a cart rumbling along the rough road, and a few moments later, an empty timber wagon came into view drawn by six immense dray horses, and driven by a brute of a man and his even more brutish assistant.

"We have come for your logs, fellow," shouted the driver, jumping down on to the ground to begin the loading up operations, with the aid of his assistant and the forced labour of the forester and his wife.

When the trees had been loaded up, the forester and his wife stood weeping, as they saw the beautiful trees being taken away, trees that the forester had cut down after a great deal of labour, trees that were now being stolen from him for the hated Prince John.

"He is stealing my trees," he moaned to his wife," and now he wants two hundred golden guineas as well. We might as well go and drown ourselves in the river, we are helpless and hopeless."

"Hush," said his wife, "don't let the men hear what you are saying, or even worse things might befall us if they report your words to the Sheriff and to the Prince. People have been hanged for less."

They watched the dray being driven off in the direction of London, and they stood there at the road side weeping and clinging to each other.

"We are ruined," sobbed the forester, "we have nothing left to live for."

Suddenly a man emerged from amongst the trees at the road side, and he said, "I have heard all that has transpired, worthy forester, but don't worry. We will help you."

The forester and his wife stared at the figure in Lincoln Green, and their eyes widened in wonderment and hope.

"I do believe that it is Robin Hood," said the man, "Yes, it is he indeed. By all that is wonderful."

"We are in such trouble," cried the forester, "what can we do, good Robin?"

"Leave everything to us," said Robin gently, "we will look after you and deal with the situation to the very best of our ability. I already have a plan in mind, so just go back to your hut and make yourselves a good meal, the Sheriff will not be back until tomorrow. Here is a small piece of venison for your meal. Roast it and enjoy eating it, and then have a good sleep, for you both look completely worn out. I will be back almost before you have opened your eyes again. Good-bye for the moment."

Robin handed over the meat that he took from a small sack that he was carrying on his back, and then he strode off along the road, waving back to the forester and his wife and grinning at them cheerfully.

He had been watching the Sheriff from the cover of the trees, and had heard every word that had been said, and now he was glowing inwardly at the prospect of the opportunity to score a point against Prince John and the Sheriff. Now as he walked along the road, he unrolled a brown robe that he carried rolled up under his arm, and put it on, pulling the hood down over his face to complete the disguise, and minutes later, he had caught sight of the horses and dray on the road ahead of him.

"Hey," he called out to the driver, who reined in the horses to stare owlishly at the figure that was hurrying up behind him. "Hey, I want a word with you, my good man."

"What do you want," growled the driver in a surly voice, scowling at Robin in a stupid kind of way.

"Where are you taking those trees," asked Robin, "to London?"

"Aye," replied the man, "to London, and a mighty long way it is with these heavy trees. I don't know why they can't be sold locally, but the Sheriff seems to have a special customer there down south, so his will must be done. I don't fancy the trip, for there are outlaws and robbers and murderers in this forest, and also on the Great North Road that leads to London, and I don't fancy my chances of getting through alive."

"Would you consider selling the trees to me for just a little more money than the London customers are going to pay you," asked Robin, jingling some coins in his purse, "I will also buy the horses and dray from you, as I am in need of some good strong horses for my own work."

The driver's eyes sparkled with greed as he realised that he would be able to keep the extra payment for himself, and only have to hand over to the Sheriff a small portion of the money that he would get for the horses and the dray.

"It's a bargain," he said, climbing down off the dray and motioning to his assistant to get down on to the ground also. Robin Hood took a purse from his pocket, and showered a glittering collection of gold coins into the drivers hands, and then flipped the purse on top of them.

"You will want something to put the money in," he said, "you might as well have the purse as well. It is no consequence to me. Somebody once gave it to me full of money, and now it is empty again. I do not need it."

Robin climbed up on to the drivers seat and whipped the horses into motion again.

He left the men standing in the road way, counting out their share of the gold coins, and he grinned delightedly at the success of the first part of his plan.

The coins had once been paid to him by the Sheriff of Nottingham when Robin was still the Earl of Huntingdon, and the coins had turned out to be forged and false coins. The Sheriff had thoroughly and completely tricked him then, but Robin had now got his own back, and he would have given much to have been a fly on the wall to watch the Sheriff's face when he saw the false coins and heard the dray-man's story.

Robin drove the dray far into the forest along a track, and then gave out a sound that was an exact replica of that of an owl's hoot. Almost before he had time to alight and un-harness the great horses, he was surrounded by twenty of his men, and he quickly told them what had happened.

"We will cover the dray with bracken and branches," said Robin, "so that the thing will be completely hidden, and then take the horses to eat their fill in that dell over there. I want half a dozen of you to stay with the horses and guard them and the wood, until I can give you further instructions. I shall be in touch with you again before night-fall."

In the meantime, the two dray men returned to Nottingham and were taken to the Sheriff's room. But when he heard their story, his face flushed with rage. When they poured the coins on to his table and put down the purse, he almost fainted, so infuriated was he when he recognised his own forged coins.

"So Robin Hood has started his tricks under his new guise," he shouted, "I should have sent soldiers with you to guard the trees. You fools and imbeciles, these coins are false and worthless, and we have lost the logs and horses and dray into the bargain. I will have you flogged for this, I will have you hanged."

He choked with anger, and sank down on to his chair again, trembling and almost weeping with the upset of the whole business.

"I will have you hanged in the forest the first thing in the morning," gasped the Sheriff at last, "I cannot have bunglers working for me. You are useless. Guard, take these men to the dungeons until the morning, and then hang them in the forest."

Some of the servants had heard the Sheriff shouting and screaming, and they also heard the name of Robin Hood mentioned. Like wild-fire, the story ran through Nottingham that Robin Hood had tricked the Sheriff, and the story was heard by four of Robin's men who had entered the city disguised, to buy bread and a few other necessaries. The story of the forged coins caused a great deal of merriment, and when the story was carried back to Robin, he roared with laughter.

"I would have given twenty real gold coins, to have been there to see the Sheriff's face, when he saw the forged coins that he once gave me," he roared, "Oh! how delicious."

The trees of the forest almost rocked with the sound of laughter, and for many a long day, the men chuckled when they thought of the incident.

"The Sheriff is hanging the two men in the morning here in the forest," said Will Scarlet.

Suddenly Robin grew serious, and he cried out, "He would go too far and try to spoil a good joke. The two ignorant fools cannot pay with their lives for my joke on the Sheriff. We will have to rescue them and send them on their way to a safe place, maybe London in the stage coach. They will never dare to come back to this part of the country again, so we shall be safe from their meddlings."

The following morning, a small band of the Sheriff's men entered

Sherwood Forest, dragging the two great brutes of men behind them on long ropes. The men howled in cowardly terror when they reached the clearing near the edge of the forest, and when the nooses were fitted round their necks, they made such a fuss that the Sheriff's men heaved them up and left them swinging there to die as fast as they could and as best they could, and did not wait to see the final moments of the two great masses of muscle.

The men swung choking and growing black in the face, near to death, when suddenly two twanging sounds were heard, and the ropes were cut, letting the men fall in two great heaving heaps to the ground. Two arrows had cut them down before it was too late.

Before they had time to struggle to their feet, two men in Lincoln Green appeared from amongst the trees, and stood by watching until the dray men were fit to stand upright and focus their bulging eyes, rubbing their stretched necks as they did so.

"A kind friend has sent us to rescue you," said one of the men in Lincoln Green, "and he sends you this money, it is not forged money either this time. We have instructions to put you on the London coach that is due to pass this way in a few minutes' time along the Great North Road, and tell you to stay in London and not to come back to this part of the world ever again."

"You can take our word for it," choked the dray driver, "that we shall be glad to get to London and away from Nottingham for ever, away from the Sheriff and the rest of his gang. We are grateful to you for saving us from death, but it was the least that could be done after the trick that had been played on us, a trick that nearly cost us our lives. Getting us to take false coins to the Sheriff, and stealing our trees and the horses and dray from us. But that is over and done with now, and the sooner the stage coach comes along, the better we shall be pleased.

A few minutes later, the stage coach drove along the road, and the driver stopped the onrush of the horses as quickly as he could, eyeing the man in Lincoln Green fearfully as he did so, scared of a hold-up and a robbery.

"Don't worry, driver," cried one of Robin Hood's men, "we are not going to rob you, we just want you to take our two friends here to London and leave them there. They have plenty of money with them, but just to speed them on their way, we will pay their fares for them."

So saying, the man of the forest handed a bag of coins up to the driver, and then helped the two dray men up on to the outside seats of the coach. A few moments later, the coach was on the move again and was soon out of sight.

Later in the day, the Sheriff made a second call on the forester and his wife. At least, that was his intention, but he found that the hut was locked up and its owners not at home.

He searched the nearby parts of the forest, but completely failed to find any trace of either of his victims.

Suddenly his horse reared as an arrow sped straight in front of its nose, and the Sheriff had to struggle to keep his seat on the frightened animal. When the horse was more or less calm again, the Sheriff dismounted to examine the arrow, and he scowled fiercely when he saw that a note was attached to the shaft of the arrow.

The note read, "If you want logs back, come along tonight to the foot of Dingle Hill. You will get logs back with interest. Signed by a well wisher to all who are needy and oppressed."

The Sheriff gave a howl of frustration and then snarled to himself, saying, "Such tomfoolery. But I will go and see what is afoot, but just for safety, I will take a few soldiers with me. Doubtless, this will be some more of Robin Hood's fancy work."

That night, the Sheriff rode to Dingle Hill with four soldiers riding behind him. When he reached the trysting place, he called out, "Hey, there. This is the Sheriff of Nottingham. I have come for the logs that you promised to me."

He stared up the smooth green slope of Dingle Hill, and then his eyes narrowed as he saw something moving towards him. It was something that caused his horse to rear and throw him heavily to the ground, and then as he raised himself on to one aching elbow, he saw his horse turning to bolt back to Nottingham as fast as it could go, and riderless, a fact that would be noticed by every citizen of the town. He was thankful that it was night-time, so that he would be able to go back on foot unnoticed with a piece of good luck.

The soldiers' horses saw their fellow creature flee in panic, and waited for no spur to urge them to move. They leaped forward and raced after the terror-stricken horse, taking their riders with them, riders who were powerless to control the frightened animals.

The Sheriff picked himself up off the ground bleeding and bruised and alone now, and then he stared in terror at the things that were coming towards him.

Rolling down the slope were a mass of ancient logs, logs that were so old and rotten that they broke up into pieces as they bumped and spun and jolted down the hill towards the Sheriff. He leaped aside as the wood-work passed him at speed, but the trees were so full of bugs and wood lice and other crawling creatures, that he was covered with dust and vermin from the moving wood. He was coated with filth and grubs and confusion, and he was so scared and angry, that he stood there in the road and screamed abuse at the countryside in general.

When the confusion had died down, and all was quiet again, the Sheriff looked up to the top of the hill and saw a group of men standing there roaring with laughter, and one of the men was Robin Hood, himself.

"What have you done with my beautiful logs," screamed the Sheriff.

"Your logs," queried Robin Hood, "I think you mean the logs that you stole, don't you? Their rightful owner and his wife took them to London early this morning, shortly after your men were supposed to hang your dray man and his companion. Your two men took the stage coach to London, by the way."

"Another of your tricks," cried the Sheriff, "you will suffer for this, Robin Hood. I will hang you and every one of your men, when I get hold of you."

"That will be quite a day for you," shouted one of Robin's men.

"By the way," called out Robin, "you are no judge of beautiful wood, Sheriff, the forester and his wife will be able to sell their own trees to a man that I know in London for twice the price that you were asking from your customer. The man and his wife will be able to buy a nice house down in the South country with the money that they get for their trees, and they will be able to live in comfort for the rest of their lives. They can live out there and grow their own produce in peace, without having every cabbage they grow stolen by you for your own table, Sheriff. They are out of the county of Nottinghamshire by now, and well on their way to London, with an armed guard of my own men travelling in disguise with them. There is not a thing that you can do about. If you tell anybody of this little business, you will be a bigger laughing-stock than you are already, Mister Sheriff."

There was indeed nothing that the Sheriff could do about it. He could not even creep to Nottingham and tell his closest friend what a fool he had been made of again, by Robin Hood.

Snarling and cursing, he turned and walked wearily back to Nottingham on foot, hoping against hope that he would be able to slip into the town and the castle unnoticed, and creep to his room to hide his head in shame beneath his bed-clothes.

Chapter VI

THE HUNT AND THE NEW MEMBER

THE sun shone bright and hotly down on to Sherwood Forest, making it extremely warm work for Robin Hood and a small band of his men who were out hunting in the greenwood. They crept silently amongst the undergrowth, seeking wild boar, pigeons, hares, deer for haunches of venison, and even an odd swan or two, rabbits, and any other edible creatures with which to feed the growing band of so-called outlaws.

Robin shot an arrow into the air from a kneeling position, and with un-erring aim, he brought down a pigeon, dead before it hit the ground.

A shower of arrows from his fellow hunters brought down twenty birds that were dead before they too hit the ground. The birds would fill the pot for a good supper for the men, and their feathers would fill pillows for their beds, pillows that Marion herself was making for them.

A sudden cry of "BOAR HO!" distracted their attention from the birds, and leaving one of the men to gather up and bag the dead birds, Robin and the remainder of his men embarked on a chase that was to take them three miles through the narrow and devious tracks of the forest in the direction of a fast flowing stream.

The hunted animal grunted and squealed as it dodged the arrows that bounded into the ground a few inches from its swerving and retreating rear portions, but miraculously it escaped death by fractions as it dodged in and out of the bushes and amongst the trees in its flight.

"The beast must bear a charmed life," shouted Robin, as he leaped over a fallen tree and almost flew through the air after the animal.

The hunt was difficult in the rough country of the wood, and progress was slowed down a great deal by the various difficulties encountered. Bog holes had to be circled, and small but deep rivulets had to be leaped across. The boar was the most elusive that they had met so far, but Robin grew more and more determined to have the animal roasted for supper that night as the chase proceeded; nothing would have distracted him from his prey now.

Suddenly the boar reached a clearing at the edge of a fast flowing stream and made a rush for the bank. It screamed in terror as its tremendously strong legs carried it forward, and then it suddenly spun into the air to fall dead with an arrow in its brain.

It twitched for a few moments, and then lay still, whilst Robin and his men drew to a sudden dead halt on the edge of the clearing to stare about them keenly, for the arrow had come from somewhere not far ahead of them, and the boar had rushed straight into its path. The arrow had definitely not been fired by any of the men in Lincoln Green.

Robin motioned to his men to keep under cover, and he himself stepped forward alone, and from behind the cover of a tree bole, he called out, "Who is there? Who has shot my boar?"

"I am sorry to intrude upon your hunting," came a stentorian voice from the opposite bank, "but the great beast was making straight towards me, and I shot it before I noticed that it was being hunted. However, it is nobody's loss, is it? We killed the beast between us."

Robin emerged from behind the tree and strode towards a precarious bridge that was merely a very moss-grown and slippery log, that was washed almost over its top by the flooding stream that was rushing brownly between its banks.

"Now we don't know who the boar rightly belongs to," called out Robin, "we drove it here where we could have killed it, but you put an arrow into a vital spot of its body, and killed it first. I'll fight you for it, if you like."

"I like it very much indeed," shouted the man, "but let us throw aside our bows and arrows and swords, and do the job properly. Let us go into combat in a civilised and friendly manner. Cut yourself a branch off a tree and I will do likewise, and then we will fight it out on yonder bridge if you like. Three falls into the water decides the winner. What do you say, sir?"

"That will suit me," replied Robin, "I will cut my branch forthwith."

He drew his knife from its sheath, and selecting a branch that bore more than its fair share of smaller twigs, he hacked the branch from the tree and swung it round several times to test it for balance and usefulness.

Robin then advanced to the centre of the log bridge and looked up at his protagonist. The man was a great giant, eight inches taller than Robin Hood's own six foot four. The man must have been all of seven feet tall, and even possibly more. He was greater in muscle than even Rough who had joined the party so recently.

The thought flicked through Robin's mind, that the man would make an extremely valuable member of the merry men of Sherwood. That was, if his loyalties lay in the right direction, or even so fine a man as this one, would be no good at all to Robin and his friends if he favoured the hated Prince John.

The man faced up to Robin and swung his branch in the outlaw's direction in a tentative manner, and Robin also took a swing that was by way of being a try out. Then the battle began in earnest.

The giant swung his branch at Robin's legs, and only a quick skip saved the man in green from crashing down into the rough brown waters of the stream. Robin swung back again, but the man maintained his balance by some supreme effort of balancing on the slippery log. Then a series of lashes from the heavy branches made both men totter until a slip of the foot on a piece of wet moss sent Robin splashing into the fast running water, and he was swept twenty yards down stream before he could catch hold of a branch that over-hung the water. Pulling himself up on to the bank, he raced back to the log to pick up his branch that one of his men had caught for him before it could be lost in the foaming water, and before the giant had gathered himself together again, Robin sent the great man crashing into the water.

The giant clung to the log, shaking it so much that Robin once more found himself falling down into the brown flood.

"Two falls by you and one fall by me," spluttered the man, as he scrambled on to the log again.

But the score was soon even, when Robin dislodged the giant by a thrust into the man's chest with his branch, a thrust that had all of Robin's weight behind it. Only a vast effort on Robin's part saved him from following the giant into the stream again.

"Two, two," shouted Robin, dodging on to dry land until the giant had climbed back on to the log again. "The next fall by either of us, will be the decisive one."

The last part of the battle was long and hardily fought, but just as the watchers were beginning to think that the battle was going to go on for ever, a tree that had been washed away by the floods the night before, swung round the bend in the stream and bumped into the log bridge, entangled itself about the four firmly planted feet, and tripped them up.

Robin and the giant both gave mighty shouts of alarm, reached out their arms to steady themselves against each other, and then suddenly went plunging into the stream locked together in a comical embrace.

The men on the bank roared with laughter as they observed the spectacle, and rolled on the grass in merriment.

Robin and the giant struggled to the bank and dragged each other on to dry land, to lie gasping and choking for a full minute, before they recovered their breath and could stand upright again.

"It was a draw," gasped Robin when he could speak again. "We shall have to cut the dead beast in half, and have half each, to be quite fair."

"By King Richard," cried the giant, "that was indeed a wonderful fight. It has done me the world of good to encounter such a good honest fighting man as yourself, sir."

He extended a great ham sized fist and shook Robin's own not so small hand in his own.

"Did you say King Richard," queried Robin keenly, looking at the man intently.

"I did indeed," roared the man firmly, "King Richard and no other, for I am all for that great King and all against Prince John, that traitorous brother of his, the man who has taken my farm and all my stock and what money I have, through sheer trickery. Because I protested and fought them off, I now have to run for my life in to the woods, being hunted in the same way that yonder hog was hunted so short a while ago. I shall have to live now, like a fugitive. So now I seek Robin Hood, as I intend to join his band and do what good I can until the true King returns to these shores. King Richard and England, that is what I stand for."

"So say all of us," said Robin warmly, "and now good friend, what is your name?"

"My name is John Little," quoth the giant, "but because of my small size and puny aspect, there are those of small humour who call me Little John. What is your name, sir?"

"I am the man that your are seeking," said Robin, "my name is Robin Hood, one time Earl of Huntingdon and called Robert Fitzooth. Now you must call me Robin Hood, and I shall be glad to have you join my little band of men. Welcome to Sherwood Forest, John Little, henceforth known as Little John."

Once more the two men joined hands, and then little John turned to pick up the dead boar by its legs, tie them together with a piece of rope that he produced from his pocket, and then sling the animal over his right shoulder as easily as though it had been a mere batch of rabbits. Then he turned and walked away amongst the trees at Robin's side, another useful and loyal member of the men of Sherwood.

Chapter VII

FRIAR TUCK AT LARGE

"Dear me," quipped Friar Tuck, "rain in Sherwood Forest, who would have thought of such a thing? I had imagined that it would always be fair summer weather here, and free from all men's wickedness and greed. Never mind, it is only a light shower, it will be over soon, and then it will be a fine day for the famous Nottingham Goose Fair. I will break my fast with a pair of fine fat trout and a crusty loaf, washed down with a flagon of ale. Then I must hurry away on my excursion. Doubtless there will be many people there ready to buy my hand-written prayers on parchment, and people who will pay me to pray for them in Nottingham. With that rogue of a Sheriff at their throats all the time, they need all the prayers that they can get, poor wretches."

He emerged from his cave by the river at Copmanhurst, and found that the gentle shower of rain had already ceased, and had scarcely dampened the grass.

He put an arm full of dry wood on to his camp fire, and soon had a cheerful blaze going, and then he cooked his breakfast and ate heartily.

After the repast, he fed the dog and the mule, and cleared everything away, carefully putting out the fire at the end of his operations.

He left the hound in charge of the cave, and left the mule tethered up securely so that he could not wander off and get lost, and then Friar Tuck rowed himself over the stream to the opposite bank in the ferry boat and was just tieing up the boat, when he heard a shout from the opposite bank.

Looking up, he saw a minstrel standing on the opposite bank, beckoning to him to return.

"Will you ferry me across," cried the man, "I am not over-fond of getting my feet wet."

"Art thou afraid of getting them clean, wandering minstrel," shouted Tuck, "I care not overmuch for travelling players and wandering musicians, they are too often minus the fare after I have laboured to transport them across the water."

"Pay to be rowed across in that miserable coffin of an object," roared the minstrel, "I'd rather try to fly across."

After a considerable argument, Friar Tuck went grumblingly back across the water, and said testily, "The cheek of some people. What gives you the right to think that I should be made a beast of burden just for your mangy benefit."

"Just for that," shouted the minstrel, a twinkle in his brown eyes, "you can carry me across on your fat back. That is, if you can manage to pick up anything heavier than a knife and fork and spoon."

"Manage to carry you," roared Friar Tuck, "I could carry two like you, one under each arm."

"Then as there is only one of me," quoth the minstrel, "you will have to be content to carry just one of me across your tiny stream."

Tuck gave a roar of anger, and picking up the minstrel, he slung him roughly over his shoulder like a sack of potatoes, and carried him across the stream, to dump him down violently on the opposite bank.

"Thank you for nothing," shouted the minstrel, giving the Friar a farthing, "that is as much as that little trip was worth."

"As you think that you are such a fine fellow," roared the Friar, "carry me back. I wager that you could not even lift my little toe, let alone my whole body."

The minstrel shouted, "I'll take you up on that, irate old Friar, I'll carry you there and back again if you wish."

He gathered his strength together, and with a great heave, he lifted the Friar up on to his right shoulder and began to carry him back across the stream. But half way across, the minstrel found with his foot, a deep hole that the Friar had known to avoid on the trip out, and both the minstrel and the Friar plunged down into the water together.

"In faith," said the minstrel, "I ought to be clean soon, for I seem to have done nothing much else lately, but fall into the water fully clothed."

"Impudent knave," shouted Friar Tuck in a voice that was so loud, that it roused every bird for a mile around, and sent them soaring up into the blue sky. "I'll have your insolent hide for that."

The minstrel picked up the stave that he had been carrying , and began to dance round the Friar, quipping at him as he did so.

"So that's the way of it, is it," roared Tuck, "all right then, my fine fellow."

He seized his own stave, and went in to a battle that made the trees almost vibrate with the noise.

The two men fought until they were exhausted, and they staggered forward into each other's arms, to hold each other up in a state of wet exhaustion.

"Enough, fellow," gasped Tuck, "I meant no harm, I was merely joking."

"So was I," replied the minstrel, "now I think we had better light a fire and dry our clothes and eat, before proceeding on our journeys."

An hour later, fed and rested and dried out, the two men had made friends, and were about to start out into the woods, when the minstrel gave the Friar a golden coin and said, "This is for all the trouble that I have given to you, good Friar Tuck. Take it and buy something that you need, if you need anything; if you don't, just keep it until you are in want. The rich pay me well, and so I give to the poor."

Friar Tuck gave him a long and suspicious look and then he said, "Like Robin Hood of good repute. Thank you kindly, friend. The coin is very welcome."

The two men then set off in the direction of Nottingham, and reached the city to find the streets full of a gay throng.

They made their way to the market square, and the minstrel wandered amongst the people, playing his lyre and singing merry songs in a good tenor voice, whilst the Friar sold prayers that he had written by hand on to pieces of parchment. Trade was brisk for the merry Friar, for his wit was keen and he kept the crowds laughing at his jokes and quips. But all through that long and busy day, he kept his eye on the minstrel who kept returning to him for a few words, and who seemed loth to leave the Friar for more than an hour at a time.

The fair grew even more gay and noisy as the evening came on, and the crowds danced and sang in the streets, and did their best to forget their troubles for the time being, under the gaily coloured lanterns that were now lit up for the special occasion.

When the evening's festivities were over and the crowds began at long last to disperse, the minstrel and the Friar retired to Sherwood Forest to rest and eat, but the minstrel was still watchful and uneasy, and he had the appearance of waiting for somebody to come along.

When the camp fire was blazing merrily, the minstrel picked up his lyre again, and began to sing at the top of his voice. The Friar pricked up his ears as he heard the words of the song, and felt a glow of satisfaction run through him, for the song was in praise of King Richard. Nevertheless, it was a dangerous song to sing in the open air where anybody in the form of an enemy might be listening.

The minstrel let his voice ring out however, almost as though he wished his song to be heard by certain doubtful characters, and when the song was finished, he went on to sing yet another song in praise of his King.

Suddenly the sound of horses' hooves were heard on the narrow path near their resting place, and the minstrel raised his voice to an even louder volume. The horses' hooves came nearer and nearer, until suddenly four horsemen and a pack horse rode into the clearing.

Friar Tuck raised his eyes to look into those of Guy of Gisborne, and he wondered what kind of a plot the minstrel was trying to get himself involved in.

Guy of Gisborne was looking far from pleased, and he roared out, "What is this, minstrel? A song about the traitor, Richard? You should be singing a song in praise of John who should be the rightful King of England."

"I am loyal to the King, King Richard the Lion Heart," cried the minstrel rising to his feet, "as every good English man should be."

Friar Tuck's deep blue eyes twinkled as he heard the words, and he secretly admired the minstrel's cheek in standing up to the much despised Guy of Gisborne.

"Those are fighting words," cried Guy of Gisborne, "so take this sword, fellow, and let us see who is the better man, you or I."

Guy took a sword from one of his men and tossed it to Robin, for Robin the minstrel was, and then whipped out his own sword and went for the minstrel without a word of warning.

"You villain," muttered Friar Tuck beneath his breath, and then he became too busily engaged in the fight to waste any more breath on useless words. The soldiers had drawn their swords and sprung from their horses, and were now circling round the hard pressed minstrel.

Friar Tuck whipped out his broad sword and took his stand at the minstrel's side, and began to use his sword in no fumbling manner. With a quick slash, the Friar caught one of the soldier's arms and cut the sleeve half off his tunic, and a further movement brought the sleeve sliding down round the soldier's sword hand. Before the man could tear himself free of the loose sleeve, Tuck ripped the tunic from bottom to top, and began to work on the second sleeve. The soldier went mad with rage, but Tuck kept on with his bantering sword play for a while longer, and when the soldier's clothes were cut to ribbons, Tuck lashed out at the man and cut his right arm so badly, that the soldier withdrew in agony, and retired amongst the trees to try to stop his furious bleeding.

Tuck stopped playing at this point, and quickly disposed of the other two soldiers, and sent them bleeding and moaning amongst the undergrowth, and then he turned to observe the main fight, for such it obviously was.

Here was no light-hearted sword play, indulged in mainly for the enjoyment of the tricks that the adversary could not deal with. Here were two men well matched in skill, and fighting desperately. Guy of Gisborne and the minstrel were fighting so furiously, that Friar Tuck began to wonder how deep the feeling lay beneath the combat, for it seemed to him that there was deep-rooted hatred between the two men, and so he refrained from joining in this seemingly private quarrel.

The fight continued fiercely for such a long time, that Tuck began to worry on his friend's account, for the man must surely be wearying by now. Tuck was determined to take over the fight before the minstrel could be injured, and so he stood with his sword at the ready.

He need not have worried, however, for suddenly the minstrel gathered his strength together and lashed out with the flat of his sword against Sir Guy's tremendously thick neck, and Sir Guy fell like an ox that had been pole-axed, to the ground.

Sir Guy lay with his eyes closed looking as though he was in a deep sleep, but his soldiers merely watched cautiously from amongst the trees, unable to go into battle against the two magnificent swordsmen.

The minstrel threw a pot full of water over the camp fire, completely dousing it, and then he took the pack horse by its bridle and gave Friar Tuck an immense wink.

"We must do as Robin Hood does," he said quietly, "and rob the rich to feed the poor. Don't you agree, good Friar?"

"I do most certainly agree," replied the Friar, his mind probing into the problem of the identity of the minstrel even more closely, the man was obviously far more important than he had seemed at first. He was above all, a terrific fighting man, and no weakling in physical strength.

The two men gathered together their belongings, and made their way deep into the forest, and had rapidly put a great distance between themselves and the soldiers and their unconscious charge.

To the weary men and their stumbling pack horse that was obviously too heavily laden, the way back to Friar Tuck's cave seemed long and arduous, but eventually they reached their destination, weary and once more tremendously hungry.

As Friar Tuck made the fire, he felt that an age had passed since he had last knelt and worked his tinder against the dry twigs.

After a good meal of bread and cold meat and ale, they unpacked the saddle horse and found that the bags contained gold coins.

The minstrel turned to Friar Tuck and said, "I hope that you are no lover of Prince John and his followers, for if you are, I shall slice you in two with my sword and throw your bits and pieces to yonder hound to eat up. My sword here, this one that Sir Guy presented to me, and forgot to ask to have it returned! Maybe his being unconscious, that little detail completely slipped his mind."

"You need draw no sword to me on that account," replied Friar Tuck, "as you should have gathered by now, I hate Prince John and all that he stands for. I got turned out of the Monastery because I would not kiss the dirty feet of the Prince himself. I got turned out, and was glad to leave a place that would give house room to a man who is a traitor to his own country, and to his own brother, King Richard."

"Say no more," said the minstrel, as he examined the contents of yet another bag of gold coins, "Sir Guy must have had a fantastic day gathering all this money for the Prince. Tax money extorted from the poor, to whom it will be returned as soon as I can find the rightful owners. He was collecting the money all day, the black hearted scoundrel, and I'll wager that he intended to keep a goodly portion for himself without telling the Sheriff. Birds of a feather flock together, and you know what kind of a bird the Sheriff is, Friar Tuck. He is a vulture."

Tuck wrinkled his brows in perplexity and asked, "How did you know all this, minstrel?"

The minstrel said, scarcely looking up, "I have ways of finding out. I have friends in the right places, Friar. I shall return the money to its rightful owners as soon as possible, as I usually do under such circumstances."

The minstrel fingered a horn that was slung from his belt, and then he raised it to his lips and gave three sharp blasts upon it. It seemed to be only moments, before the woods were alive with men, men clad in Lincoln Green and who did homage to the minstrel as though he was their much revered leader.

"Take this gold back to the camp," said the minstrel, "my mission for the day has been completed more than a little successfully, and I will join you in a little while. I have something that I wish to discuss with my friend here, and then I will be with you all again."

41

The men slipped away into the forest as quietly and as quickly as possible, and were gone as mysteriously as they had come. The minstrel turned to the Friar with a smile playing round his strongly formed lips.

"Have you not guessed yet who I am," he asked.

"I guessed a long time ago," replied the Friar, "but now I am sure of my facts. You are Robin Hood. You went to the Goose Fair to lure Sir Guy in to the forest afterwards with his gold, so that you could get it back from him. Then you would return it to the poor people who had been forced to part with what in some cases must have been their life savings."

Robin's eyes glittered as he said, "I have watched him all day, getting taxes from the stall holders and threatening them if they did not pay up. He is too much hand in glove with the Sheriff, to be decent. I had to get the money back for them, and for the old folks in the cottages that he visited this day. The man makes me sick. Tomorrow morning they will all get their money back secretly, for my men will go round Nottingham disguised as pedlars, and they will give charms away to the people, and little bags of sweets that are really the money that was stolen from them on this black and wicked day. The tax payers will find their gold back in their own hands, and no man will know how they got it. With the money that I earned singing, I will buy things for the poor people and have them given to them. Food and fuel for their poor fires, and clothes. Anything that they need."

The Friar pulled his purse from his pocket and tossed it to the minstrel, saying, "I have enough for my needs without this, good Robin. What a delightful way of life," he said, "what useful work you are doing. How I envy you all in your work."

"Why envy us," replied Robin, "why not join us? We could use a priest to guide us into a wiser way of life."

"You don't seem to need any guiding," put in Friar Tuck, "you have enough ideas of your own. But I will gladly join you, I will just gather together my own miserable odds and ends of possessions, and come along with you straight away."

He filled two great sacks, and then he loaded up his mule, and he even strapped two bags on to the back of his great hound. He and Robin shouldered the sacks, and carried the remainder in smaller packs which they carried in their hands. Completely laden and heavily bowed down, Robin said, "If this is your idea of a few bits and pieces, I wonder what your idea of a big load would be like. This stuff must be bricks and books, judging by the weight of it."

"This stuff is the same kind of merchandise that you go in for," said the Friar, "gold and coins and jewellery stolen by three thieves that I chanced to meet. They had taken the stuff from goodness knows where, and they were going to hand it over to the Sheriff. I took it all from them when I took over the cave, and sent them packing. I will tell you the story as I go along. There is something buried in the cave also, but we can come back for that tomorrow, it should be quite safe until then."

"Is this stuff to be handed back to the poor," asked Robin, smiling.

"Certainly," said the Friar, "every coin of it. It should make quite a few poor hearts the richer."

"It will indeed," cried Robin joyfully, and then the small party, both animal and human, slipped away into the forest.

Chapter VIII

MARION AND THE TALISMAN

ROBIN HOOD and Friar Tuck had made good time back to the secret encampment, in spite of their very heavy loads, and they were greeted joyfully and with much relief by the merry men, and most of all by Robin's wife Marion.

"I don't know how Hercules and Bane will agree with each other," said Robin anxiously, after a hearty supper had been eaten, "but we shall just have to take a chance on it. If the fight gets too bad, we shall have to pour water over them to stop the combat. A waterfall of ice cold water is the best way known to man or beast, to stop a fight."

Rough fed his hound until it was too full of good food to move too quickly, and Bane in a different part of the camp received the same type of treatment, and then the dogs had been let loose to find each other and make friends if possible, and with a good slice of luck.

The dogs looked at each other in surprise, touched noses, and then suddenly and surprisingly, Bane leaped away and raced into the woods with Hercules on the animal's heels. They disappeared without a trace, and were not seen again for many a long day.

A week after the disappearance, Rough said, "Bane has never been away as long as this before, but doubtless the animal will find its way back here in due course. Maybe it has gone back to the old cave."

"What about Hercules," queried Friar Tuck, "surely two strange dogs could not have made friends so quickly, two big fierce beasts like they are. Set up housekeeping in each other's company like that, it isn't natural."

"You never can tell," smiled Rough, and then he turned to his wood chopping once more, and Friar Tuck had to hurry away on some other errand that was waiting his attention.

Time went by and still there was no sign of the hounds, and because of various urgent pieces of business and sundry adventures, the matter slipped from the men's mind for the time being, apart from the minds of the owners of the hounds, and they secretly worried about their animals.

Now and again, the baying of the hounds could be heard, but nobody caught sight of the dogs, not too far away, just tantalisingly out of sight.

One bright sunny day in the autumn, Marion decided that she would like to gather nuts and berries for winter use, and as Friar Tuck and a group of the men were going fishing that day, they decided that they could act as her body guard and make the two trips into one for safety's sake as far as she was concerned.

"The best mulberry bushes are near the Great North Road," said Marion, "and as the stream runs very near the road at that particular point, you could do your fishing there and be within ear-shot of me if I needed help from you."

The men agreed to her plan, and dressed in monks' robes for a safe disguise, and set off on the little venture. When they reached the stream and the men had settled down to fish, Marion wandered off on her own with her baskets one in each hand.

"We must keep the Lady Marion in sight," said Tuck anxiously when she had gone, "so you climb up that high tree, Much, and keep a close watch on her. Don't take your eyes off her, and don't hesitate to use an arrow if she is set upon. Give us a shout the moment you even imagine that something be wrong. Off you go now."

Much climbed up the high tree, and his brown monks' robe and brown stockings camouflaged him against the tree bole and amongst the mass of green leaves. He never took his eyes off Marion as she wandered from bush to bush gathering berries and nuts, and even when she reached the edge of the road, she was still in sight.

One or two travellers on horseback rode past and exchanged pleasant greetings with her, but she went un-remarked by all who saw her, for she was dressed in the clothes of a simple peasant woman, and the sun bonnet hid her bright golden hair almost completely.

She was deep in thought as she worked, and was startled when she heard a man's voice close to her side, and glanced round in alarm. The man was completely unaware that an arrow was being aimed straight at his heart from the tree above if he made one wrong move.

"Forgive me if I startled you," said the man in a rather smarmy voice, "but I am a pedlar, and I have some beautiful pieces of dress material in my bag. I would be most obliged if you would be so kind as to examine my wares. I also have some delightful imitation Roman jewellery in the form of bracelets, and rings and necklaces. May I show the things to you?"

He stared up into her face, and craftily noticed that she had not the features of an ordinary peasant, but was obviously finely bred. When she spoke to him, her voice and accents were cultured, and his eyes narrowed slightly as he watched her hands touch his silks and satins.

He chatted to her and told her all the news of the neighbourhood, and Marion listened politely and with great interest, for he mentioned several people that she knew. But she made no more than a few brief comments, not disclosing the fact that he was speaking of intimate friends, or of bitter enemies.

She chose a deep red dress length and a small bronze bracelet, and a bundle of brightly coloured ribbons, and paid the man with a golden coin that he eyed with surprise, for the peasants always paid him in far less valuable coins when he went peddling. This strange lady was obviously something far above the ordinary run of people.

"What is your initial," he asked casually and smoothly, "I would like to give you a lucky charm with your initial upon it. Is it J or K or D? What is it, Madam?"

"M," she replied unthinkingly, for she was concentrating on a piece of lace that had taken her fancy.

"N," he put in, "N for Norma."

"Not, not N" she contradicted, "M. M for Marion. A moment later she wished with all her heart that she had lied to him, for the man had glanced at her sharply as she said the name.

His eyebrows rose a good half inch, and then he said, "Marion. Yes, of course."

He produced a box full of charms on metal chains, and chose one for her with special care. It was a small blue talisman, and had the initial M picked out upon it in glittering stones that looked almost like diamonds. They caught the light beautifully in the sun, and Marion took the talisman in her hands with a little cry of pleasure.

"Oh, how pretty," she said, "I will wear it straight away. How much do I owe you for it?"

"You owe me nothing for the talisman," replied the pedlar, "you must have it for nothing with my compliments. It is a mere nothing, I give one to all my best customers."

"Thank you," said Marion, fastening the chain about her neck and fingering the talisman with pleasure.

"Do you live far from here," he quizzed.

"Not very far away," replied Marion guardedly, "just a little way into the woods."

"It must be a lonely life for a fine lady like your good self," he put in smoothly.

"Oh, I have plenty of company," she said quickly, and then trying to make amends, added, "My husband and the farm men, and the helpers that we have in busy seasons. I do not get lonely."

He stared at her keenly and went on to ask, "whereabouts in the woods? I know of no farm near here."

"There are various small farms in the forest," she replied quickly, "and ours is one of them. There is no need for me to tell you more, is there?"

"Do you not get weary of the life here," asked the pedlar, "do you not wish to visit your friends in town now and again? See the sights and sounds of Nottingham? Have a look at the shops, or go to Church there? If you care to be here this evening at five oclock, I shall be passing in a small pony and trap that I am buying from a friend, and I can give you a lift in to town so that you can visit your friends. Then I will collect you in Nottingham later in the evening, and bring you home again. I will bring you straight to your own front door."

"Thank you," replied Marion, "but I shall be too busy to go out tonight. I have a lot of work to do."

"Nonsense," said the pedlar, "nobody is ever too busy to visit old friends. I will meet you here at dusk. I will not fail you."

The pedlar made up his pack again, and Marion folded up her new posessions, and the two parted company, and she huried back in to the woods where Friar Tuck and the other men were fishing, first making sure that she was not being followed.

Her companions looked the picture of peace and contentment as they sat fishing in their monks' robes, and nobody would ever have suspected that they were anything else than what they appeared to be.

Nevertheless, it would have been very awkward if the man had followed her back to her companions, and would have led to all kinds of dangerous complications.

Marion showed Friar Tuck her purchases and told her about the overcurious pedlar and his strange gift, and the Friar examined the jewelled initial with great interest.

"I hope that Robin will approve of my purchases," she said, "the pedlar had some really beautiful things in his pack, not the usual class of goods that pedlars usually carry, by any means."

"Nice bait," said Friar Tuck, a frown showing on his brow, "I'm not sure that I like this. One has to be so careful in this part of the world, there are spies and ill wishers everywhere."

"I am a bit suspicious," said Marion, "he said he would pick me up in a new horse and trap that he is buying today, and give me a lift in to Nottingham tonight, so that I could visit my friends. Then he said that he would bring me home later, right to my own front door. I said no, but he was most persistent and went away without going further into the matter. I am supposed to be meeting him at dusk."

"M for Marion," muttered Tuck, "I have an idea that the fellow knows who you are. He will either try to abduct you, or else take you in to town and bring you back safely as you think, but with a party of the Sheriff's soldiers not so far behind. They would dearly love to find our secret camping place, and they are hoping that you would lead them straight to the spot."

"I wouldn't dream of going, of course," put in Marion quickly, "that would be the most foolish thing in the world to do."

"Of course you would not go," replied Tuck, beaming at her, "you have far more sense than to go and do such a silly thing. But the pedlar does not know that, he thinks that you will fall into his trap, whatever it is. Now let me think. I have an idea."

He fished in silence for a while, and Marion wandered around gathering more berries and nuts until her baskets were full to overflowing, then the imitation monks who had now caught enough fish to last them for every meal on the coming day which was Friday, packed up their fishing tackle and their catch and made ready to accompany her back home, for that was now how they looked at their very secret encampment in the middle of the forest.

As the party walked away through the woods, Tuck said, "I'll wager anything that you like, that the man recognised you. Did you pay him in copper coins, by the way?"

"No," she replied regretfully, "I made the mistake of giving him a gold coin. I should have known better."

"No matter," cried Friar Tuck, "perhaps it is a good thing that you did pay him in such suspicious coinage. He was probably looking for you anyway, he had to find you sooner or later. He thinks that he has cooked up a simple plot, that will cook us all like a set of stuffed geese ready for the Sheriff's oven. I'll tell you about the plot later, when we get back to camp. We shall have to get permission from Robin Hood first of course, before we can operate, and then we can set our own little trap."

The imitation monks and Friar Tuck together with their charge, returned to the camp in great good humour as the prospect of another adventure sent the blood coursing a little faster through their veins, and Robin greeted them joyfully and was delighted when he saw the big catch of fish.

"We might be able to catch an even bigger fish tonight," said Tuck with a sparkle in his eyes. "Sit down, good Robin, and I will tell you something exciting."

But Robin's face took on a grim expression, when he heard the story of Marion's encounter with the pedlar.

"I don't like it at all," he said, "I am feeling very uneasy about the whole business. I can deal with any dangers and difficulties that may crop up for any of us and never turn a hair; but when it comes to having Marion involved, that is an entirely different matter."

"Marion will not be involved any further," put in Friar Tuck, "for I have a plan in mind that does not include her at all, may I outline what I have in mind, Robin? If all goes well, we shall be able to make complete fools of those who follow us back to the hideout."

Robin scowled, but after a few moments of thought, nodded his head in assent. "At least you can tell us what you have worked out in that crafty old mind of yours, Friar Tuck," he said.

As Tuck went into his plot in detail, a grin began to break out on Robin's handsome face, and he finally agreed to the plot being put into operation.

The band then settled down to work the thing out to the last little detail.

That evening, the pedlar waited anxiously for Marion to appear, unaware that Friar Tuck was watching him from amongst the trees.

"As I thought," muttered the Friar to himself, "my friend the imitation hermit of Copmanhurst. So he is back and in action again, no doubt trying to get his revenge on me and on the outlaws for taking his loot and his mule and dog. He has really planned his revenge, and no mistake. I shall have to settle with him for good and all, later on this evening."

After a long wait, when it was nearly dark, the slim figure of a woman emerged from the woods, a woman in a black cloak and hood and a peasant woman's dress. The diamond initial M caught a beam of light, and flashed for a few moments, and the pedlar was sure that this was Marion.

"I am very sorry that I am late," the woman whispered, putting a basket full of pies and berries and a bottle of wine into the cart, and then she climbed up on the seat next to the pedlar.

The lady pulled the hood over her face so that her features were quite obscured, and then she settled down on the hard seat whilst the pedlar whipped the horse into a brisk trot. He was in a hurry to reach Nottingham before it was quite dark, as the road was infested with highwaymen and outlaws, and he feared that Robin Hood might send some of his men in persuit.

He reached Nottingham just as darkness closed in completely on to him, and he had been so busy with his own thoughts, that he had failed to notice that his passenger had also remained silent during the whole of the trip.

"Where do you wish to be taken," he asked quietly, turning to try to peer into her face, but the hood completely hid her features from him.

"Just at the corner of this street," she said quietly, and when the cart had drawn to a halt, she climbed down, and having collected her basket, hurried up the street to knock at the door of a small cottage. Then she lifted the latch and went inside, closing the door behind her. A few moments later, a light appeared in the curtained window of the cottage, and all was silent.

"That is the house of Milkins and his wife, I think," muttered the pedlar, "I will wait here and watch and follow when the lady moves on to visit other friends."

The evening passed painfully slowly, and the pedlar began to wonder if the lady had eluded him by leaving the cottage by a back door. It was almost midnight before the door opened again, and the lady emerged from the doorway to approach him once again.

"Have you enjoyed your evening in town with your friends," he asked politely, helping her into the cart and passing her the empty basket that she had given to him to hold until she had got aboard the cart again.

"Very pleasant, thank you," she replied, "but I am weary. My friends are such chatter-boxes, that I am quite bewildered with their chatter. I feel half asleep already."

The initial on the talisman glittered in the moonlight, and a thin smile twisted the pedlar's lips, as he whipped his horse into motion again.

He drove quickly through the streets and out through the gates and on to the Great North Road again, but as he passed into the open country, he began to whistle a little tune. It was a pre-arranged signal, and there were ears ready to hear it.

He drove the horse and cart to the place where he had met Marion that morning, and drew to a halt.

"Which way do we go now to get to your home," he asked, a hint of excitement shaking his voice a little.

"I will drive now," said Marion, taking the reins from his hands and whipping the horse up into a brisk trot and then a gallop. The cart moved up a side road and into a forest track that was scarcely wide enough for the little vehicle.

The drumming of horses' hooves behind them were muffled by the trees, and both passengers made the pretence of not hearing the sounds. But the woman whipped the little horse to a faster and yet faster speed, and the cart bumped and rolled on the un-even surface of the woodland track.

The sound of hooves came nearer and nearer, but never quite caught up with them. Suddenly, Marion slowed the horse down, and the cart moved forward at a much more respectable rate. Immediately, the horsemen behind them seemed to slow down also. The woman stopped the cart and the horsemen behind stopped also.

"I could swear that we were being followed," she said, "listen to the sound of horses' hooves. I have been hearing them for quite a while now."

"Nonsense," snapped the pedlar, "you are just hearing the echoes of my own horses' hooves. You hear all kinds of strange sounds in the middle of the night in a forest, Mistress Marion."

Marion whipped up the horse again, and the cart began to move over the rough ground noisily. The sound of horses' hooves once more started up behind them, but Marion said nothing.

The ground became wetter and wetter, and the moonlight shone on the waters of a bog at both sides of the track. Suddenly they were in a small clearing, and the centre of the open space was filled in with the wettest bog that the pedlar had ever seen in his life.

"Are you sure that you are not lost," cried the pedlar in alarm, for he had begun to sense that something had gone wrong with his plan, very wrong indeed.

"Now for a bit of action," shouted the woman in a frighteningly deep voice, confirming the pedlar's suspicions. "I got deadly weary of waiting in that empty house all the evening, for my friends had removed to London several days ago. However, now we can start moving again."

The pedlar sprang up in his seat, to stand motionless for a few moments before plunging dead to the ground below. An arrow from Tuck's bow had caught him full in the chest over his heart, and brought an end to his miserable criminal life. He fell with a wet thud in to the bog and began to sink horribly out of sight, the arrow being the last thing to disappear. But nobody had time to watch this sudden burial of the dead.

The woman drove the horse and cart out of sight into the woods, for the vehicle and the horse would be very useful to Robin and his men in their work.

Moments later, the horsemen who had been following the cart found themselves ambushed by the men in Lincoln Green. and the battle that followed was one of the fiercest that they had indulged themselves in up to date. For twenty minutes the battle raged, and as time went by, more and more of the Sheriff's men found their last resting place in the waters of the hungry bog.

Fortunately the men in green suffered no severe wounds, for they were fresh and rested and ready for the fight, whereas the Sheriff's soldiers had been at work all the evening on some other of the Sheriff's business enterprises, and had then been ordered to follow the pedlar into the woods to capture the hideout of Robin Hood and his men.

The shock attack by the men of Sherwood had thrown them off their balance, and the quick deaths of twenty of the soldiers had caused them to lose their nerve not a little, in fact quite a lot.

After a hard fought battle, the remainder of the men threw down their arms and threw up their hands in surrender. But Robin Hood did not trust them in this move, for he knew that they would have some trick up their sleeves in the manner of all the Sheriff's fighting men.

The shock had not lessened the soldier's cunning, and they were determined to find the secret hideout that they were convinced could not be far away from the battle ground. They had intended that Robin and his men should take them prisoner, and take them back to camp, but Robin knew that this was what they had been hoping for when they found that they had been led astray by the woman in the horse and cart.

Robin and his men tied the men to their waiting horses so that they could not make a move to control the animals, and then the men of Sherwood whipped the horses so that they turned tail and fled back to Nottingham, to run headlong into a small band of horsemen that were following after them. The fresh horsemen were the Sheriff and six of his personal bodyguard.

Robin and his men heard the confusion, and guessed what was happening.

Simon Trim, who had played the part of Marion for that evening's performance, picked up the dress that he had borrowed from Marion to wear as his disguise for the night for the little trip with the pedlar into Nottingham, and threw it into the bog, for it was tattered and covered with the blood of the Sheriff's men who had staggered with shock when the person that they thought had been Marion, turned and attacked them, sending two of them into the bog to their deaths before they could gather their wits together.

Friar Tuck beamed at the success of his plan, but Robin said, "All is not over yet, good Friar. I hear more horses approaching. Let us set a further trap for them."

He tied a rope across the path a foot above ground level, and they all hid once more behind the trees. Half a minute later, the small body of horses and their riders rode madly up the path to trip over the rope and to go crashing into the waters of the bog.

"I hope that you will enjoy your dip in the lake," cried Robin, "good night, Sir Sheriff and your merry men. Good night."

Robin and Friar Tuck and the men melted away into the forest, leaving the Sheriff and his soldiers to get themselves out of the bog as well as they could, and to gather up their dead and wounded for the return trip to Nottingham.

"This is the second time that you have tricked me," screamed the Sheriff into the forest, "but I will have your blood yet, Robin Outlaw Hood."

But the woods were silent.

It was much later in the night when Robin and his men returned to their base camp, and fell wearily on to their beds to sleep the sleep of the just and the adventurous.

The following morning, as they were enjoying a late breakfast, they heard the sound of hounds baying away in the distance.

"They are sending the dogs to seek us out," gasped Much. But the men had scarcely jumped to their feet and seized their swords, when who should come racing in to the camp but the hounds Hercules and Bane, followed by a whole pack of dogs that were exact replicas of themselves, a pack of very young puppies, no less.

"Hercules is back," cried Friar Tuck joyfully, throwing the remains of a leg of lamb on to the ground, and receiving his out-sized pet with open arms. Bane rushed up to Rough and licked his bearded face with a rasping sound that could be heard twenty yards away.

"Good girl," said Rough, "I wondered where ever you had gone to. So you eloped with that rascal Hercules, did you? Now you have brought your new family back to join the men of Sherwood."

"Girl," gurgled Tuck, "no wonder they did not fight on sight."

Robin Hood roared with laughter and then he said, "It must have been a case of love at first sight."

Then he collapsed to the ground under the onslaught of the eight new puppies, and rolled around trying to escape from the violently licking tongues of the new pack of hounds.

"Welcome to the camp," Robin cried, "Master and Mistress Hercules and family."

Chapter IX

THE MAGICIAN

LITTLE JOHN did not have a great deal of difficulty in pushing his way through the packed streets of Nottingham, for the crowds on the narrow pavements divided quickly to let the seven foot giant march through on his way.

51

The men glanced at him quickly, admiring his great muscled arms and his vast shoulders, and the ladies looked at his pleasantly smiling and good-natured face. He marched to the market place, and then paused to look around him, and try to locate the sounds of merriment that had just reached his ears. Somewhere the people were roaring with laughter, and obviously enjoying themselves, and the sound of laughter was something that was getting more and more rare in Nottingham as the days went by. Then on a small platform, he espied a gaily clothed figure of a magician who was obviously entertaining the crowds most successfully, and in the best possible manner.

The great man strode across the square and stood behind the small crowd, enjoying a good view of the proceedings over the tops of their heads, and after he had watched the show for a few minutes, he realised that the magician was extremely good at his work. Trick followed trick in rapid succession, and the audience gasped in amazement, for it was impossible to guess how some of the tricks had been done. When he produced a beautiful little white rabbit out of a hat, the crowd shouted in delight, but when a young man appeared from nowhere when the magician flicked aside a cloth, the crowd began to wonder if this was real magic and not just a conjuror's set of tricks.

To finish with, the conjuror asked Little John to go up on to the platform to help him with a trick. He joked about John's size and told the crowd that the little lad might one day grow to the size of a man, and he then asked John's age.

"Thirty two," replied Little John.

"Thirty two indeed," gasped the conjuror, "and what stopped you from growing, little man?"

The crowd roared with laughter, but Little John took it all in good part and joined in the hearty laughter.

The conjuror then did a trick with a hangman's rope, and Little John heard him mutter very quietly beneath his breath, that he would dearly love to have the head of Prince John within the rope.

Little John raised his eyebrows quickly, as he heard the muttered words. When the show was over, he whipped off his peasant's hat that he was wearing as part of his disguise, and made his way through the crowds to collect money for the conjuror, whilst the conjuror also made his rounds. Between them, they collected a very tidy sum indeed. Then they packed up the conjuror's tricks, and went to a pie shop to buy themselves some food, and the two men and the conjuror's boy found a quiet spot where they could sit and eat. A spot where there were no long-eared listeners to overhear their conversation.

"What is your name," asked Little John, making great inroads into his second pie.

"My name is Wellenough," said the conjuror, "and I certainly was well enough until that accursed Sheriff booked me to entertain the guests at one of his banquets. The guests took far too much to drink, and became quite drunk, and that oaf of a Guy of Gisborne got roaring drunk and spoiled my show altogether. The Sheriff turned really nasty when I dared to complain, and not only refused to pay me my fee, but went so far as to confiscate my house and all my furniture and all my money, and that was quite a tidy sum. That man is nothing more than a licensed thief, hired by the Prince to grab anything that he can lay his filthy hands upon."

Little John's face flushed with rage as he heard the story, and he asked the conjuror how he managed to live now, and where he slept.

"How do I manage to live," replied Wellenough fiercely, "I live by travelling from market square to market square, performing in the streets, and begging for my bread as you have just seen. Instead of performing in great houses for the gentry and in theatres as I used to do, for the Sheriff has turned everybody against me, or at least they dare not employ me after what he has done. I have a good mind to go into Sherwood Forest and join Robin Hood and his men, for I feel that my special talents might be put to good use by the men of Sherwood who have all suffered at the hands of the Sheriff and his overlord. As for where I sleep, I sleep in barns and hedge bottoms and anywhere that I consider safe."

"I think that it could be arranged for you to join the band," said Little John with a smile, "I know Robin Hood very well, and I have an idea that you can join as soon as you like. I will take you there this evening, and introduce you to the great man. How about that, friend Wellenough?"

The conjuror's eyes sparkled when he heard this.

"Could my assistant join as well," he asked, "for the Prince hanged his father shortly after his mother died, and took all their property, such as it was. That man's sins are certainly black indeed."

"Of course he can come with us," said Little John, "I will meet you here this evening after the market has closed, and take you back with me to Sherwood. But do not breath a word of this to anybody, or we may be followed by ill wishers, and then there would be real trouble for us all. We have to move carefully, as you will guess."

That evening, Little John collected his two new recruits, and took them back with him into the forest, with the conjuror's properties loaded on to a small cart and drawn by a well-kept horse. Robin greeted the man joyfully and Wellenough and his assistant were immediately sworn in as members of the band.

After a hearty supper of roast venison and sweet pasty, Robin insisted that Wellenough should put on a show for them, and the conjuror was delighted at the prospect of entertaining the famous men of Sherwood by having them as his audience.

He went through his tricks, and then as an added treat, he said, "Lady Marion and Gentlemen. I would now like to perform a trick that is quite new to this country of ours. It is a rope trick that I learned to do in an

Eastern country when I was abroad recently. I saw it performed by one of the greatest magicians that the world has ever known, and now I am going to do this trick for you now, as he honoured me by showing me how it was done."

He built up a great bonfire and then placed a basket on the ground and began to play a tune on a weird set of pipes that he had brought back with him from overseas. Slowly the lid of the basket raised itself and then a rope rose slowly up into the air, rigid and straight, up and up into the night sky without any visible means of support. The conjuror then put his pipes down on to the ground and clapped his hands. The boy came running towards him, and the conjuror ordered the boy to climb the rope, but the boy pretended to be disobedient, and chased round and plagued the conjuror so much that he pretended to grow very angry. Then the boy teased him and raced up the rope and of sight. A moment later, he gave a scream and pieces of meat began to fall down on to the ground. The rope went slack and fell down on to the grass, and the boy was gone. Then Wellenough pretended to cry and wave his hands about in despair.

"Alas," cried Friar Tuck, "our young friend has been turned by magic into a set of lamp chops, or should it be boy chops."

Suddenly there was a shout, and the boy ran out of the woods from behind them, and ran straight into the conjuror's arms, and Wellenough embraced him joyfully and the men of Sherwood applauded mightily.

"That should have been the end of my show," said Wellenough, "but I have just one more trick up my sleeves. My magical lantern trick. Simple but effective."

He fixed a white sheet against some trees, fixed up a lighted lantern, and slipped a piece of painted glass in front of the light. Instantly on the white sheet, appeared a picture of a mighty treasure trove. Piles of bags of gold and silver coins, and a heap of jewellery that looked as though it should be worth a King's ransom.

The men cheered when the show was over, but Robin Hood was strangely thoughtful, and he called Wellenough over to him when the man had once more packed up his tricks.

"I have an idea," said Robin, "a shipment of gold and silver coins is being transferred from a certain man's house that I know of, to the Sheriff. The treasure is quite substantial, and when the Sheriff has taken this money from the farmer, he will not have a penny piece left, never mind the money that the Sheriff will take in taxes, and therefore the Sheriff will take the man's farm and all his stock in that crafty little way that he has."

"That is indeed bad," said Wellenough, "there is no end to the man's greed and wickedness."

"I only heard the news today," said Robin, "and I have been wondering how to deal with the situation. The hoard is going through the forest tomorrow night under quite a heavy guard. A lot of blood would be spilt if we fought for it. Is there no other way we can get it?"

"Maybe I could use my magic to get it for you," said Wellenough cheerfully," please let me try."

"How would you get it," asked Robin Hood, "just wave your magic wand and conjure it away into our caves?"

"No," replied Wellenough with a smile, "but I have got an idea that would do away with bloodshed and fighting."

They talked the matter over and after a while, a plot was hatched that was both cunning and clever, and as safe as possible.

The following night, a body of horsemen rode through the forest along the roadway, with several pack mules heavily laden beside them. They reached the very centre of the forest, when they were accosted by a man in strange robes, the robes of a magician.

"If I did not know for certain that Merlin was dead," said the leader of the band, "I should have sworn that you were the great Merlin himself."

"I am not Merlin," said Wellenough, "but I am certainly a magician, and I am wondering whether you would like to see a few of my best tricks or not, if you are not in too much of a hurry."

He produced a handkerchief and a glass and did a simple trick with it to whet the men's appetites for more, and they sat on their horses intrigued by his display.

"We will tether our horses to these trees together with the pack mules," said the leader, "for we have come a fairly long way far too quickly, and could do with a little break for supper and for a rest. But we will see your tricks first, Master Magician."

They followed Wellenough into a nearby clearing, and sat down to rest whilst he laid and lighted a bonfire and began to perform his tricks. He began his display with his special rope trick, and then went on to a display of fire work tricks that banged and sparkled and made the forest ring with their noise, and then on to a trick that demanded that the boy should bang on his drum and play tunes on his pipes, or shout and sing whilst at the same time getting the men to join in with the music. The men became so intrigued with the magic, that they completely forgot about the pack mules that they had tethered nearby, and only hidden from the road by a few bushes and trees. They were not to know until much later, that the pack mules and their horses had departed in some mysterious way, and they were to imagine that the animals had been spirited away by the magician's magic. They were never to know that Little John and a group of men in Lincoln Green had come under cover of all the noise that Wellenough and his assistant had been making, to take the treasure and the animals away, the pack mules had been needed to transport the treasure, and the horses had been taken to prevent the men from following the men of Sherwood on horseback and overtaking them. The horses were the property of the Sheriff anyway, and so Robin and his men considered them to be fair game.

The audience sat entranced by Wellenough's show, and applauded every trick with a loud clapping of their hands, and shouts of amazement, adding to the general commotion.

To end his performance, Wellenough produced a glass ball that he claimed to be highly magical, and held it up for the men to see.

"In this magical ball," cried Wellenough, "I can see great treasure. Bags of gold and silver and piles of valuable jewelry. I see it all, and if you watch the direction of my hand, you too will see the treasure. Look away amongst the trees there, and you will see a great treasure all piled up and ready for you to collect. Go and get it, my good men, and thank you for allowing me to entertain you all. Good night."

He had been pointing behind him along an avenue of trees, and there at the end of the forest way, was the treasure waiting for the men to collect, or so they thought. Wellenough had placed a sheet at the end of the long avenue, and his assistant Tinker who was hiding away amongst the bushes with the magical lantern, was throwing the picture of the treasure on to the screen.

The men rose to their feet and hurried along the avenue that was far longer than they had imagined that it would be, away into the forest with the light of the bonfire behind them.

Wellenough suddenly doused the fire with buckets of water that he had previously filled and hidden amongst the bushes, and when the fire and its comforting light had so suddenly been extinguished, they felt vastly alarmed as they were plunged into blackness, by magic as they thought.

The treasure trove seemed far away from them, and weirdly unreal, and it seemed to move farther away as they moved onwards, but this was only their imagination. They kept their eyes fixed on the hoard in case it should suddenly disappear from sight, and their clumsy feet ripped and stumbled over the rough ground and the tree roots as they progressed.

But they were concentrating too much on the treasure and not enough on where they were putting their feet, for suddenly and with a cry of alarm, they stumbled and plunged down in to a deep hole that had a bog at the bottom of it. The men fell in up to their waists and began to sink, even deeper, and it took them a good twenty minutes to get out of the mess and another ten minutes to get back their nerve and their breath. When they looked about them again, the treasure had gone.

"That magician has tricked us," shouted the leader of the gang, "we must hurry back to our mules before he magics them away."

The gang stumbled back through the forest to the place where they had left their mule train and the horses, to find that they too had completely disappeared. Horrified, they searched for their charges, but could find nothing.

"The Sheriff will hang us for this," gasped the leader, "and if we try to catch the magician, he will bewitch us all. He may send us up that accursed rope of his, and send us crashing down to the ground again cut up into pieces, as he did that boy. The best thing that we can do, is to get as far away from Nottingham and the forest as we can, and never come back again."

That night the Sheriff grew more and more angry when the men did not arrive with the farmer's gold, and the next day, when he sent out a search party, his men failed to find any trace of the men and the treasure, or of their animals.

The next day, the farmer received a surprise visit from a small party of men dressed in dark brown cloaks, cloaks that covered their Lincoln Green suits completely, and he was amazed when he discovered that their leader was none other than Robin Hood.

When Robin told him what had happened, and that he had brought back the gold and silver that had been stolen from the farmer, the man wept for joy, for he had thought that he was about to be ruined by the Sheriff.

"On top of your personal treasure," said Robin, beaming with happiness, "I will give you enough money to pay any taxes that the Sheriff may demand from you at this time. Also you can buy one or two more cows quietly, and add them to your own stock without any fuss."

The farmer threw his arms round Robin Hood and wept for joy.

"Any time that you or your men want rest or refuge or help," he said, "let me know, and I will do all that I can to help you. If you are on the run, come straight here, and I will hide you in my cellars until the danger is past."

"Thank you, friend," replied Robin Hood, "I will remember that."

Chapter X

ROBIN MEETS ALLAN-A-DALE

ROBIN HOOD stopped dead in his tracks and raised his head to listen to a voice that was ringing through the forest in glorious tones, and he smiled as he heard that the gay tenor voice in the distance was singing of love and happiness and the beauty of this glorious summer's day.

"There goes a very happy man," said Robin to himself, "what a wonderful voice. I should very much like to meet its owner, unless he is one of Prince John's men, then I should wish that his tenor voice would turn round in his throat and choke him. But only one of our own King Richard's men could sing as well as that, I'm sure."

Half an hour later, he actually did come face to face with the young man and he spoke a few words of greeting to him. He saw that the young man's face was handsome and pleasant, and a happy smile was lighting up his face. Then with a wave of his hand, the young man was off with his bow and arrow to hunt for a hare that he had seen bounding away down the path ahead of him, and Robin turned to go upon his own way also.

Robin almost forgot the little incident, but a week later, he met the young man again. Robin was shocked to see the change in the man, for now the handsome face wore a most woebegone expression, and dark circles were under his eyes to tell the tale of many sleepless and miserable nights since Robin and he had last met.

The tenor voice was not raised in song, and the man scarcely raised his eyes to Robin's as they came face to face on the pathway.

"I am collecting money to give to a poor peasant woman whose hut was burned down by the Sheriff yesterday," said Robin, "all because she had no money for the taxes, and now she has no home and is sleeping in a cave in the woods until we can find money to buy her a new home and what furniture and clothes and food she will need."

The young man raised a miserable face to Robin Hood and said, "Alas, I am as poor as she is. I have but five shillings and a wedding ring left, and the ring is waiting for the finger of my true love. Yesterday I was to have married Lorna Demaine, but she was been taken from me by force; and today in a few hour's time, she is being compelled to marry a very rich but extremely ancient old Knight."

"What is your name," asked Robin sympathetically.

"My name is Allan-A-Dale," said the young man, "I am a poor minstrel with only the gift of song to earn me my bread. Lorna loves me, and is willing to have me, penniless as I am. I can also shoot an arrow or wield a sword, but that is all that I can do. I have no money or property, and I have lost the clerking job that I had in Nottingham, because I refused to work for the Sheriff."

"My name is Robin Hood," said the man of Sherwood, "I have even less reason than you to love the Sheriff and his master, Prince John. You say that your bride is to be married in a few hours. Can we get there on foot? Is the place of marriage far from here?"

"We can get there in time," sighed Allan, "but what is the use? What could we do if we did attend the ceremony?"

"Lend me your harp," said Robin, "I have an idea. Now let us hurry to the church, before it is too late."

Robin and Allan hurried through the forest and into Nottingham to the church where Lorna Demaine was to be given in marriage to the ancient Knight, and they found the church filled with a fine congregation, all waiting impatiently for the bride and the groom to arrive.

"Wait at the back to the church," whispered Robin to Allan, "and hide behind yonder pillar."

Robin then pulled his brown hood over his face as far as he could, and strapped his robe round his body, so that his green tunic would be completely hidden, and then he struck up a chord on the harp and began to sing a wedding song as he wandered up the aisle.

He recognised the Bishop of Peterborough standing on the altar steps, frowning and tapping his foot impatiently, and still he looked no more impatient than did the rest of the congregation gathered in the church on that not very happy day.

"My Lord Bishop," cried Robin Hood, "as the bride and her groom are a little late in arriving, may I please sing a few merry wedding songs to keep the congregation happy until the blessed pair do arrive?"

"Very well then," said the Bishop impatiently, "but you must stop playing and singing, the moment that the bridegroom arrives. Now get on with your songs before the people get really annoyed over the delay."

Robin struck another chord on the harp, and began to sing in a rich baritone voice, and soon the congregation were listening happily to the music.

Suddenly the sound of trumpets outside the church heralded the arrival of the bridegroom, who stumbled up the steps and into the church, to peer dimly up the aisle before setting out on the long walk, assisted by his best man who was even older and more feeble than himself.

They took their place at the side of the altar, and still Robin went on playing and singing, in spite of the various signals from the Bishop. After another long wait during which time Robin went on singing and playing lustily, the bride arrived on the arm of a distant relative. Her eyes were red with weeping, and she walked up the aisle, halting at every other step.

"Keep your face up and stop weeping," said her escort, "you are not going to your execution."

"I might just as well be," sighed the bride, as she drew to a halt before the altar.

Still Robin went on singing and playing at the top of his voice.

"Silence, minstrel," shouted the Bishop, "can you not see that the bridegroom has arrived?"

"I can see no bridegroom," put in Robin, staring about him and peering up the aisle to the door of the church, "I shall go on playing and singing until he arrives, but I do not see him yet."

"He is standing beside the bride before the altar," shouted the Bishop angrily, "now cease your noise, man."

"That old man," gasped Robin in shocked tones, "he is no bridegroom, he is the bride's grandfather who has got into the wrong place in church. He could never be the bridegroom to such a fair young maiden."

"Look," roared the Bishop, "that elderly gentleman is the bridegroom, he is my own brother, and he is going to marry Lorna Demaine. I am her legal guardian as her parents are both dead, and she is going to marry my brother. When she is twenty-one years of age, she will inherit great wealth, but until then, I tell her what to do. Now do you understand?"

"I understand only too well," replied Robin tartly, "there is money in it, is there? You are going to see to it that your brother will get his hands on it, and he will let you have a goodly sum of it too, I'll be bound."

"How dare you," screamed the Bishop, his face going purple with fury.

Robin turned back his cloak and threw back his hood, and then he blew his horn, knowing that his men were not far behind him, for he had left a message pinned to a tree by an arrow before he had accompanied Allan to the church, and he had seen that one of his men had slipped from amongst the trees to collect the message.

Suddenly the church seemed to be filled with men in Lincoln Green, and as the Sheriff and the bulk of his fighting men were away on a business trip, there was little danger of Robin and his men being outnumbered. Nevertheless, the action was a risky one, and everybody knew it.

Allan-A-Dale hurried up the aisle, and took the bride's hand, and smiled warmly at her.

"I refuse to marry them, the banns have not been called," cried the Bishop.

"In that case," roared a great voice, "I myself will call the banns."

So saying, Little John strode down the aisle, picked up a surplice that was lying on one of the choir stalls, and put it on in spite of the fact that it was much too small for him. He managed somehow or other to sling it round his shoulders, and then with one mighty step upwards, he was in the pulpit and facing the amazed congregation.

In ringing tones, he read out the banns seven times in all, and then he said, "If three times is not enough, seven times should make sure of the job. If the Bishop still refuses to perform the ceremony, we have good Friar Tuck with us, and he will gladly take the Bishop's place."

"Nothing of the kind," muttered the Bishop, fumbling with his robes, "I will perform the ceremony, of course. Why not?"

Out of his eye corner, he saw that Robin Hood had slung the harp over his shoulder, and was now fingering his bow, and the Bishop remembered hearing tell that Robin could fit an arrow to his bow and shoot it straight at the target, quicker than any other man living.

"Now go ahead with the service," said Robin Hood firmly, "or it will be the worse for you."

"All right," said the Bishop, "but you will all be very sorry about this. I will get my own back, and so will my dear heartbroken old brother there."

The ancient Knight had retired to one of the pews, and was now sitting down, looking very much relieved that he was not going to be forced to marry a young and frisky young woman who would plague and natter the life out of him.

Robin placed an arrow in his bow and pointed the arrow at the Bishop's breast even more definitely than he had been doing previously.

Without any further argument, the Bishop picked up his prayer book, and began the service, and the congregation stood whilst the words were being read out, and the responses were being made. Then the Bishop declared them man and wife, and blessed the ring on the bride's finger.

When the service was over, the happy pair withdrew from the church, covered by Robin's arrow, and those of his men at arms, and then the couple rode away on horseback, followed on foot by Robin and his men, ready to shoot down any trouble that might come their way.

"It will scarcely be safe for either of you to be out and about for a while now," said Robin, a worried frown on his sunburned forehead, "so what say you both to spending your honeymoon in Sherwood Forest? We will guard you and look after you both, and you can go home when you are ready."

"I have no home to go to," sighed Allan-A-Dale, "never was there a bridegroom so ill prepared as I am."

"I have no home now," said the bride, "I have lived with the Bishop and his wife, and the creaking old brother of his, ever since my parents died. I cannot take my husband back there, and I do not inherit my own house and my fortune for a long while yet. But if Allan would care to join the men of Sherwood, I should be glad to throw my lot in with his. I would rather live in Sherwood free for the rest of my life, than live under the heel of the Bishop and the Sheriff. My money used to be kept at a friend's house, and he paid me good interest on it. Now I can draw on it whenever it is needed, and you are welcome to all of it, to use as you think fit. It can be used for the good of us all."

"This is the happiest day of my life," cried Allan-A-Dale, "please let me have my harp back, good Robin, and I will sing a wedding song as we go along."

So Allan-A-Dale and his bride came to live in Sherwood forest, and they were to have many happy years together in the greenwood, and have many exciting adventures.

Chapter XI

THE BISHOP'S REVENGE

WORMAN stood before the Bishop of Peterborough and stared at him across the untidy desk in the Bishop's own sanctum, his eyes smouldering with fury. Years ago, Worman used to work for the ex-Earl of Huntingdon, but as his loyalties leaned towards Prince John and the Earl had been very definitely for the King, the two men had indulged in a violent quarrel that had ended in a sword battle with Worman coming out worst in the end. Worman would bear the deep scar on his cheek for the rest of his life, a scar that the Earl had planted there with a nick of his sword play.

The man now worked for the Bishop as his scribe, and general news gatherer, for the Bishop liked to know what was going on in the city of Nottingham, so that he could make full use of it for his own benefit. Worman had a nose for any movements of money or treasure, and the information invariably found its way to the ears of the Sheriff and his men, and Prince John reaped the ultimate reward.

But now something other than money was preying on the Bishop's mind, the little matter of revenge on Robin Hood and his men for the trick that they had so recently played upon him over the matter of Allan-A-Dale's wedding.

"I have a plan," snarled the Bishop, "and I want you to make all the necessary arrangements, Worman."

Worman's eyes glinted maliciously, but he listened in silence, glad of a chance to get his own back against Robin, if at all possible, and also in any way possible.

The Bishop gave a thin smile that did not reach his cold eyes, and then he went on to say, "Gather together four men whom we know are secretly in favour of that Richard person, as opposed to our beloved Prince John, and make it know that the four men are to be hanged in Sherwood Forest the day after tomorrow. Robin Hood will hear of this, and we will make very sure that he does hear of it, and we can then ambush Robin and his men when they stage their rescue operations, and I am very certain that they will put on such a rescue."

The Bishop and Worman plotted the whole operation out together down to the last detail, and then the scribe went away to make all the necessary arrangements, and see that the arrests were made.

To make doubly sure that Robin should hear of the hangings, Worman sent out the Town Crier the following morning, to cry out the news to the people of Nottingham, and he hung about the streets to see what effect the announcement would have on the various people of that crushed city of Nottingham.

He thought that he espied one or two of Robin's men amongst the crowds, and smiled an evil smile as he saw the startled expressions on the faces of the suspected men of the greenwood. Then Worman made his way to the house of the city hangman, and made all necessary arrangements with him also.

"You will be accompanied by three men who will form the hanging party," said Worman to the hangman, "and carry out your duties in the clearing beside the stream just off the main road that runs through the forest. The place that we always use for hangings outside the city. Then when the men are hanged and dead, just leave them there, and we will do the rest. The hanging will take place at ten of the clock tomorrow morning."

Outside in the street, a beggar stooped to fasten the lace of his shoe just outside the hangman's window, and then stood there for a while, begging coppers from passers-by in the street. When Worman took his leave of the hangman, the beggar slipped away into the crowds and disappeared from view.

62

Later that evening, Robin Hood's men brought the news to their chief, and Robin frowned as he listened to their words.

"This is no ordinary hanging," he said quietly, "it is the first time that I have heard of the Town Crier being sent round the streets to give out the news. I have a feeling that a trap is being set for us. So we will forstall the plan, and I will go out first thing in the morning and put a little plan of my own into operation. I will work it all out in my mind, and give you your instructions later on after supper. I fancy that we shall soon have quite a battle on our hands. As the Sheriff is away at the moment, I rather fancy that the Bishop of Peterborough is at the back of this. Worman went to see the hangman, and Worman is the Bishop's scribe. The Bishop has a good reason to hatch a plot against me, and putting two and two together, I think that we have marked down the instigator of this new outrage."

Robin sat in silent thought for quite a while, and then he went to join his men at their evening meal, and when they had all eaten, he gave them their instructions and then went to his cave to take a good night's sleep in preparation for the next day's work.

He would have to have all his wits about him for the task, and he knew it. He also knew that he could succeed in his task, but he offered up a prayer to ask for success on his scheme all the same. Then he slept solidly for several hours, to wake to hear the birds singing in the forest, and the first streaks of dawn light showing across the sky.

It was deadly cold when Robin washed in the stream, but he soon warmed up again when he had got a good breakfast inside him, and then he set off through the forest to put the first part of his plan into operation, accompanied by a small body of his men, six men including himself.

The hangman and his three companions together with the three victims were at the same time making their way to the place of execution, glancing anxiously about them as they went.

"We are very early for the hanging," said one of the men, annoyed at having been roused from his warm bed hours sooner than needed, by the nervous hangman.

"Do you think that I am going to give Robin Hood a chance to put an arrow through me in broad daylight," said the hangman, "I want to get into the forest and the job done, before Robin and his men are about. The last hanging party were found with arrows through them, and I don't want the same thing to happen to me. This hanging matter has been made very public, and the time broadcast by that fool of a Town Crier. Ten o'clock in the morning, indeed. The wood will be alive with Outlaws by then, and we should not have a chance. Let's get the job done before it is properly light. Make haste man, make haste."

The woods were silent as the hangman and his three companions, and the four victims made their way to the hanging place, and more than once they stopped dead to listen and peer about them, but they could see nothing.

"We are being watched," said one of the escort, "and followed too, I'll wager. I have no stomach for this job.

What happened next was something that went with the precision of a well drilled military manoeuver. Some sets of brawny arms reached out from amongst the trees and seized the hangman and his three companions, and muscular hands went over their mouths to stop any shouts that the men might make, then ropes were bound round them and black hoods pulled down over their heads. A few moments later, the men lay helpless on the ground, and they never saw that their attackers were clad in Lincoln Green. Firm hands removed the hangman's robes, and a simple smock was pulled over his head. Then the men were hauled along to the hanging place, and the ropes that they had been carrying over their shoulders, were taken from them and slung over hefty tree boughs. The men struggled, but found themselves powerless to do anything, and they were heaved up on to their feet. Two minutes later, they were hanging from the trees as dead as mutton, and their own victims were weeping with relief at their own deliverance.

The trembling men were escorted back into the forest, where they begged to be allowed to join the band of outlaws, for they would never be able to go back to Nottingham. Indeed they had no families or homes left to go back too.

"If we went back to Nottingham," said one of the men, "we should surely be caught and really hanged this time, in a cell under the castle. So please let us join you, and then we can give you lifelong service in repayment for saving our lives."

So the band grew in number by four more men.

But Robin was anxious and on edge, for the hanging had taken place hours before the appointed time, and if the Bishop had planned an ambush, his own fighting men would not be due in the forest for some time yet.

Suddenly he paused in his tracks and said, "I am going to dress in the hangman's clothes and go back and pretend that the men have just been hanged. You take the intended victims back to camp and feed them, and let them sleep, for I'll wager that they slept very little last night. The forest will be alive with my own men, watching for the expected invasion, three of you can come with me and pretend to be the other three members of the hanging party. It was a good idea of Much's there, to change the clothes of the victims for the hanging party, for the disguises will be needed now. Three of you put on the escort's clothes, and let these poor men wear your Lincoln Green. We can swear them in later, when we have completed this little piece of business."

So when the clothes had been changed, Robin and his three men went back to the hanging ground, and settled down to wait for whatever might turn up, their swords concealed beneath their robes and their bows and arrows hidden inside a hollow tree.

The birds were singing merrily in the trees now, and the sun was rising into the sky, warming the air and making the general atmosphere far less chill and forbidding. But the four swinging figures on the trees cancelled out the cheerful atmosphere, and Robin and his men felt chilled as they began their long wait.

It seemed hours before they heard the first sighs of movement, and then everything seemed to happen at once.

Four men in Lincoln Green rushed into the clearing and drew their swords and began to attack Robin Hood and his escort, muttering under their breaths as they did so, "There are fifty soldiers coming up the path, we should have a good fight, good Robin."

The captain of the small army drew his sword and rode down on to the four men in green, shouting as he did so, "Back to the woods, Master Hangman, we will protect you."

Those were the last words that he ever spoke, for Robin drew his sword from beneath his black robes, and caught the captain full in the throat with the point of the weapon as he galloped by. The captain fell with a crash to the ground, dead before he hit the turf. As Robin pulled his sword free, he heard the swish of arrows along the path, and the screams of dying men. The Bishop's ambush was failing under a shower of arrows. Five minutes later, it was all over. The dead littered the path, staining the grass a deep red, and those who remained uninjured, helped their stricken companions back to safety. Robin and his men stood and watched them go, and when the woods were clear of the Bishop's men, Robin took stock of his own men and was deeply relieved to find that nobody had even been scratched.

"Now go back into the woods and keep me covered," said Robin, cleaning his sword and putting it back in his scabbard, "and I will resume my role of hangman, and my escort will have to play their part for just a little while longer. Hurry now, for I hear the sound of horses approaching at quite a fast pace."

Moments later, the men in Lincoln Green had disappeared, and the hangman and his escort remained with the dead men.

A short while afterwards, a small party of horsemen rode into the clearing, with a white and shaken Bishop in their midst.

"Mr. Hangman," cried the Bishop, "what is the meaning of this? What had gone wrong? All these dead soldiers! How did it come about that they did not kill you also, those men of the underwood? Tell me what has happened?"

Robin laughed and pulled off his hood, crying, "My Lord Bishop, is your conscience troubling you at last? There is your hangman up on that tree together with his escort, they have been dead since dawn. They did their hanging too early, and your men arrived much too late to do anything for them. Your ambush failed completely, and the bait you set is not safe in Sherwood Forest, dressing itself up in Lincoln Green. So if you want to collect them and have another hanging party, you will have to come yourself to fetch them. I can hardly imagine you doing that, my Lord Bishop.

You have walked straight into my hands, have you not? I could have hanged you and your little party of horsemen, but that would have been sacrilege. Therefore, I will take your scribe instead, my old friend Worman."

"Never," cried Worman, clinging to the reins of his horse feverishly as though they would support him and fend off the danger that he was in, "don't hang me, Lord Huntingdon, please."

"Lord Huntingdon," cried Robin, "that title was taken from me a long while ago. I was not thinking of hanging you, but if you would care to fight me with your sword, that would indeed round off today's sport. Off your horse and out with your sword, Master Worman."

Worman gave a cry of terror, wheeled his horse round, and fled back along the forest path to Nottingham.

"All right," shouted Robin, "leave it until you are in the forest again some time, maybe you will feel more in the mood for it then."

Robin glanced at the Bishop again, and then took a second look, the bantering look disappearing from his face.

The Bishop was staring about him in terror, his face livid, his eyes flickering round as he observed the dead men that had been his own soldiers, then he said, "Some of these men are only young boys, and some of the others have wives and children. I am responsible for sending them to their deaths. All this was my idea. Oh, what have I done? Many times I have been behind the Sheriff and his schemes, but I never realised until now what such a battle could be like. All this death, Oh, God forgive me."

Robin motioned to his escort, and they turned and left the Bishop with his dead . . . and with his conscience.

Chapter XII

THE WITCH OF THE WATERFALL

MARION breathed in the warm sweet air of the forest, and a feeling of well-being flowed through her veins. She wandered off into the forest, observed at strategic points by the men of Sherwood from the look out points amongst the tree branches, look out points that were never for one moment left vacant for a single moment of the night or of the day.

Suddenly a great black bird swooped down almost on to her head, startling her so much that she cried out in alarm. The bird flew closely round her in three great circles, and then flew along beside her, hopping from branch to branch. It was so near to her, that the watching archers dare not risk taking aim, in case they missed their target and hit the precious Marion instead.

Marion stared at the bird for a few moments, and then curiosity over-

66

came her, and she wondered how the raven came to be in the forest, a type of bird that was so rarely seen in these particular parts of the forest. She walked towards the stream and then turned to walk along its banks until she came to a waterfall that she had often seen from a distance, but now she intended to view it from a nearer vantage point.

Her Lincoln Green suit and trousers gave her perfect freedom of movement, and she clambered along the rough path to the foot of the waterfall, and then she once more saw the ominously dark shadow of the bird against the surface of the waters, and then once more the bird flew towards her as though tempting her to travel on a little farther towards the waterfall.

The bird perched on a rock a little way up the fall, and then it suddenly disappeared, leaving Marion to look carefully about the surface of the water searching for the body of the bird that she was convinced had got drowned.

Then she heard a croaking sound, and saw the flutter of dark feathers through the waters of the fall, and decided to go up and investigate for herself. Maybe the bird had built a nest in this particular place as birds were famous for seeking out the most odd places in which to build their nests. But behind a waterfall was a little too strange, and Marion decided to investigate the mystery for herself.

She climbed up the rocks at the side of the waterfall, and then she paused and sniffed, for the aroma of wood smoke came to her clearly from behind the fall.

She paused and wondered, asking herself who could be camping out in such a damp place. Maybe there was some sort of a cave in the rocks.

The raven was watching her from a rock perch, and then it turned and disappeared into a hole. Several times it put out its head as though inviting her to enter, and then it vanished from view again.

Marion clambered farther up the rocks, and then she saw the mouth of a cave on a ledge, and a curl of smoke coming out of the entrance. Somebody was living in the cave, and she made up her mind to get to the bottom of the mystery. Robin ought to know about this strange inhabitant, whoever it might be. Friend or foe.

She moved cautiously into the cave, fearing some trap, and then she stared in amazement at the scene before her.

The raven was now perching on the shoulder of its owner, and its owner was a witch sitting on a low stool up to a fire that blazed in the centre of the cave. Most of the smoke was rising through a hole in the roof of the cave, but a small portion puffed out through the entrance from time to time.

The witch stared at Marion with unblinking eyes for a few moments, and then she raised a claw-like hand and made a few strange motions with it.

Marion felt herself suddenly growing numb, and fought against the feeling, the spell that the old witch seemed to be trying to cast over her.

"Who are you," croaked the witch, "and where do you live?"

Marion had the strange feeling that all this was a dream, and that she would wake up soon in her own cave, with Robin sleeping soundly at her side.

"I live in a hut with my aged parents in the forest," she said, her lips so stiff that she could scarcely move them. Then she began to ramble incoherently.

The squeak of the raven brought her to her senses suddenly, and she made a dive for the cave entrance. The old woman made a dive for her, but rolled off the stool and fell forward on to the fire, sending cinders and ashes flying all over the floor. The old crone gave a wild scream, as she felt herself being burned, and Marion took the opportunity of rushing out of the cave, to scramble down the rocks to the side of the brook again.

She reached the bank of the stream and stood trembling as though she was suffering from intense shock, and then she saw two of Robin's men rushing towards her, and she pulled herself together and smiled at them.

"Are you all right, Lady Marion," asked one of the men, "you look very pale."

"I am quite all right," she replied, "but I have had a bit of a shock. I will tell you all about it as we go back home."

She stared up at the waterfall again, and saw the witch with the raven on her wrist, hurrying back into the cave mouth under the waterfall. It was this sight that made Marion realize for certain, that the incident had really happened and was not just part of a dream.

On the way back to the camp, she was alarmed to find that the raven was following her, it was flying from tree branch to tree branch above her head obviously and strangely tracking her.

She arrived back at the camp to find Robin indulging in one of his rare leisure moments, sitting on the grass and leaning his back against a tree bole. Thoughtfully, he was chewing a piece of grass.

He jumped to his feet when he saw that she was being escorted by two of his men, and that she was extremely agitated and pale. She kept glancing above her as she entered the camp, and Robin glanced anxiously upwards when he heard a harsh croak and a sudden beating of wings as the raven flew away into the forest, back the way that he had come.

She sat down besides Robin, and he took her hand and smoothed it between his own great sunburned hands, looking at her with great anxiety.

"Have you fallen and hurt yourself," he asked quickly.

"No, I am unhurt," she replied, and then took a horn mug of water from one of the men and drank it gratefully. "I am not hurt, but I will admit that I have had quite a shock, and a very peculiar experience."

She sat down on the grass to regain her breath and her strength, and then quickly and concisely she told Robin exactly what had happened, and his brows creased in thought.

"You are sure that you did not tell her the locality of our secret camp," he said quietly.

"I am positive that I did not," she said, "I gave her an entirely wrong story about myself, and you were never mentioned. But she was such a queer old woman, that she made my skin creep, I'm positive that she is a witch. That raven seems to be almost human, and the way that it followed me back here was really uncanny."

"Could you find the cave again?" asked Robin quickly.

"I could go straight to it," replied Marion, "I have often wandered at the side of the stream near there, and have noticed the waterfall from a little distance away, but today I was attracted by the strange behaviour of the raven, and that was how I found the cave. She tried to cast a spell over me, but I somehow or other managed to shake it off, and never lost my senses completely."

"You remember everything then," put in Robin.

"I remember every single detail most clearly," replied Marion, "I knew everything that was going on around me. I remember her falling into the fire and burning herself a little, I took the opportunity to run away. I remember Much and Kearton running towards me when I rested on the grass afterwards, and I remember seeing the old witch with the raven on her wrist looking down at me from the ledge, and then turning and going back into the cave. That convinced me that I had not dreamed it all up. I remember that dreadful old bird following me back to camp, but I felt very clear-headed by then. She did try to bewitch me, I'm sure, but I managed to fight off the feeling."

Robin stared at the grass before him for some moments, and then he said, "We will look into this matter together. She may be a witch, or she may be a spy, you never know these days with Prince John probing round with every means at his disposal. If she is both a witch and a spy, she could be an extremely dangerous person indeed."

"I can easily show you the way," said Marion quietly. "I would like to get to the bottom of this mystery myself."

"When it is dark tonight," said Robin, "we will both of us go to visit your witch friend, and see what she is up to. We can take a covering of men, in case we are attacked, but I have a feeling that other tactics will be used in this particular instance. Something far more subtle than fighting, something more deadly and dangerous too, possibly."

That night, the clouds banked up as though they were trying their best to help Robin and Marion in their venture, and the night was very black indeed.

Marion and Robin led the way through the forest, and Wellenough the conjuror followed behind, wondering how his magical tricks would fare against the black arts of what was probably a real witch. Behind them came a small body of men in Lincoln Green, and the trees were swarming with archers, with weapons at the ready in case a sudden battle broke out. Then half a mile from the cave, the party stopped dead, and the men hid themselves amongst the bushes at each side of the path.

Robin, Marion, and Wellenough wrapped black cloaks around them and pulled the hoods down over their faces, and then, walking doubled over with rough staves to help them along, made their way to the waterfall. Just the three of them with the bodyguard well hidden from sight.

The raven screamed when it saw them, and a few moments later, the dark figure of the witch appeared above them on the ledge.

"Who is there," croaked the old woman, "who is it?"

"It is old Mother Wellenough and two friends," rasped the conjuror, "we would like to meet you, we have some information that will be of great interest to you."

"Who are your friends," cried the witch, the raven screaming round her head in circles, "what are their names?"

"Mother Marble and Mother Haggard," replied Wellenough in his disguised voice, "we have come a very long way to meet you. May we come up into your cave, and then we can talk freely?"

"Come right up," cried the witch, "I will fetch a burning brand to light you on your way."

She disappeared to return a few moments later, with a blazing brand in her right hand, and helped them to climb up the rocky path to her hideout. A minute later, they were inside the cave and warming themselves at the fire that was burning brightly, and sending weird shadows against the walls.

"I myself am a stranger in these parts," said the witch, "but I have a mission to perform. I came here specially to find the outlaw of Sherwood forest. I have to find him, as I have a message for him, a very special message."

"I will tell you where he lives," croaked Wellenough, and he proceeded to give her the directions for reaching the hiding place of the outlaws, directions that were completely wrong and misleading. "We also are strangers, but I happen to know exactly where the brigand lives."

"He is certainly a villain," croaked the witch, "and he has done many a disservice to Prince John, who should be the rightful King of England now. But that cursed Richard has too great a hold over certain people that we could mention, and John will never rule in peace as long as that Robin Hood is around."

"He certainly will not," replied the disguised Robin forcefully.

The witch gave a dry and choking cough, and wiped her streaming eyes on a filthy piece of cloth that she dragged from amongst her black and rusty clothes.

"Does your cough trouble you," asked Wellenough, pulling a bottle out of his pocket, "try a sip of my special cough cure, good mother, it will ease your trouble."

The witch reached out a claw-like hand and seized the bottle, then she took a deep swig of the liquid, licked her greedy lips and took yet another great gulp of the stuff. She blinked her eyes and then began to chatter away under the influence of the strong brew that Wellenough had concocted for this special occasion.

The effect on the old woman was to loosen her tongue, and she began to chatter away at top speed, telling them how she had outwitted Lady Marion that morning, and got her up into the cave.

"I got no information out of her this morning," croaked the hag, "and she pretended to be some person other to the Lady Marion. But I knew better. She will be curious and return, then I can really get her into my power, and get all manner of secret information from her, she need not think that she can get the better of me. I knew she was lying to me this morning, I knew it."

The raven screamed and flew in mad circles round the cave, before settling down on its mistress's shoulder again.

"Morgan is restless tonight," said the witch, "he knows that we are expecting especial company, and I think that our guest is arriving now. I can hear him."

The old woman rose to her feet and struggled to the cave entrance, with a blazing brand in her gnarled old fist.

The appearance of the man in the tiny cave sent a thrill of excitement through the disguised visitors, and they slouched down lower into their shabby black robes, and pulled their hoods farther down over their faces.

The man was Desmond of Gisborne, cousin and confidante to the hated Guy of Gisborne, and Robin and Marion stared at him curiously, wondering what strange business could bring such an important man to a witches cave. His purpose could not be a good one, as Desmond of Gisborne was known to be one of the most evil and sadistic of all Guy's followers. His cruelty made him the terror of the peasants, and his sins were legion against them.

"Well, old witch," he said, "how are you getting along? Have you any news for me yet, to take back to our dear Guy? He is itching to find out where Robin Hood's hideout is, and since a party of his guests were robbed by the outlaws four weeks ago, he is even more in deadly earnest about finding the thieves' lair and killing them all off. With a tasty bit of torture beforehand, eh? Guy can raise enough men to wipe out the entire band of outlaws, at a few days notice."

The old witch brought him a stool to sit on, and Robin sincerely hoped that the rickety piece of furniture would break under his weight and go crashing down into the fire.

"We have a good idea where the hideout is, of course," said Desmond, "but we do not know the safe way there, the back doors where we could creep in and take them all unaware."

Desmond rubbed his cruel hands together and rocked precariously on the stool, whilst Robin watched this uncertainty of seat hopefully. His toe itched to give the stool a helpful push, but he restrained himself with difficulty.

"The secret camp must be extremely well guarded. It must be," said Desmond, chattering on, "for the forest is swarming with Robin's men. But if we could get there unseen, we could wipe them all out and take Marion prisoner and take her back to Guy to be his bride. He still wish to have her for his wife."

Robin clenched his fists and gritted his teeth together, but was silent by sheer force of will power.

"You should have been here this morning and you could then have taken the lady back with you," chortled the witch, "she was right here in this very cave, and I fooled her. She pretended to be somebody else, but I knew better. But better still, I have three friends here who are also witch's, and although they say that they come from a long way off, they have been able to tell me where the hideout is."

Desmond stared at her agape, and then his eyes glinted as she went through the directions to the lair of the outlaws, that her visitors had just given to her.

But she had scracely stopped speaking, when he shouted in a rage, "You fool of a woman, they have told you a lie. The directions that they have given you are wrong. The directions that they have given you, lead straight into a bog. I know that, because that is exactly where Guy's men got stuck when Robin Hood and his men robbed them four weeks ago. You old beldam, you idiot. As for Marion, she will have told her husband about this hideout."

The witch glanced at her three visitors curious, and was just about to speak when Desmond cried out, "Who knows what will happen now? They may be setting a trap for us at this very moment."

The man stared about him wildly, and it was at this point that he saw the three visiting witches crouched in a far corner of the cave near the entrance.

"Who really are these people," he shouted, "they have heard every word that we have been saying. Who are they really, you old fool?"

"As I told you," she croaked, "they are witches and have come from afar and wished to meet me. I did not realise that I was so famous."

"Famous," he almost screamed, "famous for what? You are not even a real witch, you just have certain powers, and they are not very strong. You could not even bewitch a mouse, let alone Lady Marion. She was fooling you, don't you know that? She found out more about you than you would ever dream, old woman, I'll be bound."

"You said that you would pay me well if I could get news of Robin Hood," screamed the old woman, "and I did get some information for you. You are just trying to trick me out of my money."

The witch made a dive for the man, screaming that she wanted the fee that he had promised to give to her, and he struggled to hold of the clawing and scratching old hag. The woman had amazing strength, and the raven helped her by flying into the man's face and pecking at his eyes. Then suddenly he struck her a blow that sent her staggering across the cave, to fall in a heap against the cave wall.

He turned in a fury and dragged the hood from Marion's head, and stared for a few thunder-stricken moments at her features, and then he let out a roar of anger that sent the raven screaming round the cave in a madness of circles. Then the man turned in the direction of Robin Hood, and reached out his hand.

Robin sprang to his feet in a rage and threw off his robes, to grapple with Desmond in a death struggle. There was no room for sword play, and Robin whipped the dagger out of Desmond's belt and threw it out of the cave doorway, where it got caught up in the curtain of water outside and was washed away downstream.

The battle became a trial of strength, and Robin seized his adversary's hands in his and forced Desmond back and back and back, until the two men were staggering and turning on the ledge, with the slippery rock beneath their feet and the waterfall behind them.

Suddenly the raven flew, like an arrow at the back of Robin's head, but Robin ducked quickly out of the way, and the bird found itself attacking the face of Desmond of Gisborne. The man threw up his hands to protect his face, gave a wild scream as he felt his feet slipping away beneath him, and then he plunged out through the waterfall to land with a great neck-breaking crash on the rocks below.

The raven also took the death plunge, and ended a blood-stained heap of feathers on the rocks below, to be washed away a few moments later in the flooded waters of the stream.

"My bird," screamed the witch," my lovely bird. I must catch him before he dies on the rocks and in the water."

She flung herself wildly out of the cave entrance, and into the waters that roared down in front of the cave mouth.

The three watchers from above, stood on the ledge and watched the black figure swirling about in the waters of the fall, and then they heard her death scream as she hit the rocks, a yard from the body of Desmond and the handful of black feathers that he still clutched in his hands.

Robin and Marion and Wellenough moved shakily out of the cave and back down the rocky path to the grass below, and sat down to recover from their shock, and to breath in the fresh air. When they had recovered themselves again, they looked about them and found a crowd of friendly faces looking anxiously down at them.

The men of Sherwood feared no mortal enemy, but witches and black magic were quite another thing.

Quickly Robin explained what had happened, and then Marion said with a smile, "Now Guy of Gisborne will have to find other means of finding out where our hideout is, and he will have to try a lot harder than that to get me into his clutches."

"He won't love us any more for cheating him out of his objective this time," said Robin seriously, "it will only serve to make him the keener to get the better of us. The death of Desmond will stoke up even more the fuel of his hatred for us. We shall have to be even more guarded than ever now."

Chapter XIII
BLONDEL BRINGS BAD NEWS

THE years had flowed on almost unnoticed since Robin Hood and Marion and the merry men had gone to live in Sherwood forest, for they had been too busily engaged in their adventurous work to notice the passage of time. It was enough for them to know that it was either spring with the work of clearing up after the winter, summer with its gloriously hot weather and the plentiful supply of food which the forest gave to them, the softly tinted autumn that was even more glorious in the heart of the forest itself than anywhere else on earth, or the cold hardships of barren winter when the hunting for food became extremely difficult and the game and birds that they did manage to catch were at their lowest as regards health of fatness. The wild boar that roamed freely in the forest was at its most dangerous, and often the hunters found that they themselves had become the hunted, and more than one man in Lincoln Green had to make a wild rush to climb the nearest tree with a maddened wild boar at his heels, its tusks tearing at the bark of the trees that the men had climbed.

Fishing was not the easiest of tasks, and the waiting time was a cold and chilly business indeed.

But eventually spring would come round again, and the hunting would improve and the general eating would be risen to a much higher standard.

The men had lived in the greenwood for many years now, more than many of them could remember, when on one particularly green and promising spring day, a troop of extremely weary and war-worn soldiers rode through the forest.

Friar Tuck was returning from a fishing trip when he came across them drinking the fresh waters of a stream.

"Good Friar," said the leader of the men, "I believe that you are Friar Tuck."

"I am indeed," said Friar Tuck, eyeing the uniforms of King Richard on the men's backs, "I am Friar Tuck."

"Have you any idea where Robin Hood might be living in the forest," asked the leader of the men, "I have urgent and very serious news for him regarding our beloved King Richard. I must see Robin as soon as possible, for we need his help."

Friar Tuck raised his bushy white eyebrows, and stared hard at the stranger.

74

"Do my eyes deceive me," he said in breathless wonderment, "or am I looking at Richard's own minstrel friend, the faithful Blondel? Are you indeed Blondel?"

The expression on the old man's face was so pathetically hopeful and expectant, that the stranger realised fully that here was a man that he could really trust.

"I am Blondel," he said quietly, "but do not let the fact be known, or we shall all be dead men in no time if the news reaches Prince John's ears that I and my followers are back in England."

The old man was quite breathless with excitement as he said, "I will tell nobody the news, beyond Robin himself. I will take you straight away, to a place where you can meet Robin in safety, without risk of attack from the Prince's men. Come with me, I will lead the way."

Friar Tuck led the little band of men into the forest, and along so many winding tracks, that Blondel and his followers quite lost their bearings and their sense of direction. But eventually they reached a small and very secluded glade that Robin frequently used as a secret meeting place, and then Friar Tuck gave three short blasts on a silver whistle that he wore on a chain round his neck, the same chain that carried the weight of the gold cross that he always wore to show that he was a true man of God.

They had to wait a little while, and then suddenly from amongst the trees apeared Robin Hood himself, with a small band of his men around him.

He glanced at Friar Tuck, and then turned his attention to the men who were now laid resting on the warm grass, with their horses tethered and grazing near by.

Then Robin Hood stared harder than ever at Blondel, and first of all an expression of disbelief flickered across his sunburned face, an expression that slowly grew into one of hopeful joy. Tears ran down his face as he suddenly strode across to the man with hands outstretched.

"Blondel," he cried in a choked voice, "if it isn't my old friend Blondel, King Richard's own friend and minstrel. Where is the King? Where is he? Is he safe and well?"

"He is alive and well, and comparatively safe at the moment," replied Blondel, "but the wars went badly for him, as you will know. There was much treachery amongst those who were supposed to be fighting at his side, and finally when the war had been lost, the Archduke of Austria played a treacherous trick on him, and arrested him. Now he is holding our King prisoner at the Archdukes castle in Austria, and holding him for ransom. An extremely large ransom, that the duke imagines that nobody will ever be able to afford to pay. If the ransom is not paid within twelve months' time, the King's life may be in graver danger than it has ever been before."

"This is indeed bad news," cried Robin, "but at least, the King's life in not in immediate danger as it was when he was at war with the Saracens. We have at least that much to be thankful for."

"I was divided from the King in the last battle," explained Blondel, "and was extremely anxious at first, as I thought that he had been killed. We sought his body, but could not find it. Then we heard that he had been taken prisoner, and I have spent many weary and anxious months searching for him. I finally located him in Austria, and I was able to have a few words with the Archduke himself, and that was when he told me about the ransom."

Robin drew his friend to a mound of grass, and when they were seated comfortably with Friar Tuck sitting on the grass at their feet, Robin Hood motioned to Blondel to go on with his news.

"He tried to take me prisoner also," went on Blondel, "and even had me arrested. But I managed to escape from the soldiers, and I got away into France and to the coast with my friends here. We then booked our passages on a small fishing vessel owned by a man who is making a small fortune, smuggling the King's soldiers across the channel; back into England. A brigand of a man, but at least, he got us back home safely."

"You must be careful not to fall into the hands of John's men, or they will kill you," said Robin anxiously, "and don't forget that the Sheriff is for John, as are most of the Sheriffs in England. I could tell you a thousand things that the Sheriff has done for Prince John, and they would be a mere trifle, compared to everything that he has done to help John and to go against Richard. He is an evil man. But what are we to do about the King?"

"As you may have guessed by now," said Blondel with a smile, "I have come to beg for money, the ransom money, Robin. A vast sum, but if we go about it the right way, I have a feeling that we may possibly manage to raise the amount. Indeed, we must get the money, all of it."

Blondel then named a sum that made Robin Hood whistle in amazement.

"That is a King's ransom," he said, using a catch phrase, and then he smiled a little, "but that is indeed what it is. A King's ransom."

"I heard in Nottingham only yesterday," put in Friar Tuck, "that Prince John is spreading the news that King Richard was killed in battle several months ago. He will now try to be proclaimed the rightful King of England in Richard's place. What a fine brother John is, for sure, a traitor, and a black-hearted one at that."

"He cannot be proclaimed King without proper evidence," put in Blondel, "even Prince John could not get away with that, however hard he tries."

"He will try hard enough," said Robin sourly, "But I will help as much as ever I can, we must redouble our efforts to collect contributions in a manner of speaking, from travellers going through the forest, from willing and un-willing alike, for everybody must give everything that they can afford, and more. Those both for and against Richard, and I feel sure that I know most of his friends and enemies by now."

"I will go on my way," said Blondel, "but I will be back in one month's time to see how you have been getting on, and to tell you my news."

"We have quite a collection of gold and silver and other treasures," said Robin, "and the King can have all of that, we keep a good reserve fund to use when an emergency arises, and there will never be a greater emergency than this one, I'm sure. Send one of your men to the spot where you first met Friar Tuck today, and give three blasts on this silver whistle, and one of my men will come and act as escort to some place in the forest where we can talk privately."

Robin handed a small whistle to Blondel, and sent some of his men for food and drink for the weary travellers. Then whilst the guests ate and drank, Robin and Blondel talked seriously about various matters concerning the King and his fortunes of war.

The following morning, Blondel and his men made their departure, and Robin set to work with renewed energy collecting money from the various travellers through the forest. Highwaymen found themselves relieved of their illicit wealth, footpads and common thieves had to give up their gold, and the wealthy travellers with leanings towards Prince John found themselves the unwilling contributors to Richard's cause, everything that they had with them that was of any value at all, even their horses so that they were forced to finish their journeys into Nottingham on foot.

One day, Robin received the news that the Sheriff was having a large convoy of stolen treasure brought along the Great North Road, and the informant said that although the treasure train would be heavily escorted, Robin and his men could easily overcome the enemy and take the treasure. Only fifty men would guard the convoy, and Robin now had several hundred men under his command.

But the Sheriff had played light with his talk of only fifty men, for he sent an escort of two hundred heavily armed fighting men along, knowing by long and bitter experience, that Robin Hood would be sure to try to take the treasure. The Sheriff was growing older and much wiser, under Robin's indirect methods of training.

This was one of the few occasions when the Sheriff got the better of Robin Hood, for the soldiers in charge of the convoy were disguised and travelling in small groups, and as they chose a market day for the transporting of their stolen goods, the road in to Nottingham was very busy indeed, and it was impossible to distinguish the legitimate travellers from the disguised soldiers.

In a rather unfreqented part of the woods, some of the disguised soldiers slipped away into the shadows, and when Robin's men made what attack they could, the results were a disaster for the men of Sherwood.

Several of the Sheriff's soldiers died from arrow wounds that they received when they shot their own arrows up into the trees at Robin's men, but many of the Hood men were taken prisoner.

Owing to the mixture of the general public on the road, the men of Sherwood became confused as to what was their legitimate prey and what was something quite different, and that was the passing of private members of the general public along the road.

They dare not shoot many arrows, and there was so much screaming and shouting on the road from the women and children, that sword play was not to be thought of. Action was cut down to below a workable minimum. The fact that some of the Sheriff's men were disguised as women with heavy baskets of gold on their pack mules, did not help matters at all.

One of Robin's men brought news of the taking of prisoners to Robin who was watching in frustrated rage high in a tree, and he ground his teeth as he was forced to hold back his planned attack. He stormed as he saw the muddle in the road below him.

Silently he gnawed at a clenched fist as he saw some of his men being bundled away, mixed up with the holiday crowds who were going to Nottingham for the market day. He almost wept as he watched the passing from his hands, of treasure that was to have formed a great part of King Richard's ransom.

Then he cooled down as he realised that this was merely the beginning of the adventure as far as he was concerned. He would have to find some way to retrieve his men, and get the treasure after all.

To make matters even more infuriating, the Sheriff had incorporated a cattle stealing expedition with the movement of the stolen treasure, and he was having the cows driven in to the market to sell, to raise more money for the ever open and clutching hands of Prince John. The Prince's appetite for money was endless, his greed insatiable.

Robin slipped on a brown cape that he carried in a roll on his back ready for instant disguise if needed, and pulled the hood down over his face, and then he mingled with the crowd, after having given a message for Marion to one of his own men who was waiting on the ground near by. Robin then tried to find a friend who would be only too willing to give him what news he posessed.

It only took a few minutes for Robin to find a friend, and draw him to the road side pretending to gossip with an old aquaintance to cover his movements. Then they walked slowly along together, as though indulging in normal pleasantries.

"I've lost some of my men amongst the crowd," said Robin, "I'm afraid the Sheriff will be entertaining them for a while, until I can retrieve them from his dungeons, or whereever he takes them to. Another thing, I see that the Sheriff has stolen some cattle again, I would dearly like to know where he is taking that horde of beasts and all those packs of treasure. Have you any idea where he is going to hide it?"

"He has a new hiding place, they have been saying here today," said the man, "I heard some of the Sheriff's men saying a way back there when they were having difficulty with one of their mules, that they were not looking forward to having to drive the stupid beasts all the way to Wakefield. It appears, Robin, that ever since some of your men got into the Sheriff's vaults when that gentleman was having a particularly heavy drinking party, and got away with some stolen gold, that the Sheriff has been using the vaults under the house of George-A-Green in Wakefield. George is said to be a hearty fighter, and rumour has it that he is a great supporter of Prince John. But that is only hearsay, of course."

"George-A-Green," muttered Robin, "you surprise me. I always thought that he leaned towards Richard, but of course, I could be wrong. Loyalties change in some people. George-A-Green, the Pinner of Wakefield. I have heard also that he is a mighty man with his stave."

"He keeps some of his prisoners there too," said the man, "as Nottingham Castle is now no hard nut for a certain Robin Hood to crack. I hear that the said Robin Hood has quite a few friends inside the castle now, and the Sheriff is having increasing difficulties in telling tother from which, as the saying goes. So."

Robin gave a smile but said nothing.

"A new hideout has been proved to be necessary," said the man, "and that is doubtless where your own men will be going, friend. The long walk to Wakefield."

"Are you going to Wakefield, by any chance," asked Robin.

"I was thinking of going that way after today's market day," said Robin's friend, "I am supposed to be doing a little job of work for Master George, so if you have a message for any of his ... er ... household, shall we say ... I could see that the words you send would reach the correct ears."

Robin grinned delightedly under the cover of his hood, and said, "Tell my men to do whatever George asks them to do, whether it be transporting treasure, or stealing cattle, or anything else of that nature. Tell them to pretend that they are weary of working under Robin's despotic and dangerous rule, tired of winters spent out under the trees of Sherwood Forest, and ready to settle down to home life again in a nice little town like Wakefield. I will be getting in touch with them myself soon. Tell them to keep their ears open and their mouths shut, and just be as little trouble as possible. Pretend to work for the opposite side, and in that way, they could be extremely useful to our present very good cause. They will know what I mean."

Robin walked a little farther along with his friend, and then he slipped away unnoticed back into the greenwood, and back to the camp.

That night Robin gathered together a large number of his men, and they secretly plotted out a plan of action regarding the saving of the prisoners, and the obtaining of the vast treasure, together with anything else of value that they could carry away from the house of the Pinner of Wakefield.

The following day disguised as a cattle drover and armed with a small band of fat cows that Robin had kept in the greenwood for his own use, he set off on foot for Wakefield. News had reached him by word of mouth, of a cattle raid that the Sheriff's men were to make on a poor farmer that same day, and he decided to join them under the pretext that he had stolen the cows now in his posession, and wished to sell them quickly to somebody who would not be too averse to buying stolen property.

The long walk to Wakefield with the cattle was far from unprofitable as far as information gathering was concerned, and a few days later, Robin arrived in that pleasant little Yorkshire town in the company of some of the Sheriff's men who were in charge of some cattle that Robin knew well, cattle that had obviously been stolen.

The leader of the small gang worked his way round the city until he came to a well wooded meadow, and there the tired cattle were turned loose into the field to graze and drink from the silver clear stream that ran through it, and to rest and fatten up again. Robin kept his hood pulled well forward, and he had changed the tone of his voice for this particular adventure, so that even his vocal tones would not be recognised.

The leader of the men took him to a small hut at the edge of the field, and they were just about to enter, when they heard angry voices inside the small building, and drew back to listen. As Robin glanced about him, he recognised one or two of his own men who were entering the field at this moment, but they were careful not to recognise him. His brown robe and hood were familiar to them, as it was customary to disguise in this way when the men of Sherwood had any spying to do. The red cord belts were a distinguishing mark to the men of the band, and the small red and white stitch marks around the hood completed the secret markings.

"Where is the money from the last lot of cows you sold for us, George," said an angry voice inside the hut.

"Alas," cried a voice that obviously belonged to George-A-Green, "but that thieving rogue Robin Hood sent some of his men along, and they robbed me of the money before I could get it to my secret hiding place. It was quite a large sum of money, but I will get it back for you, or die in the attempt."

"You will die if you do not get it back," shouted the other man in a fury, this is not the first time that you have made excuse, and you have never recovered the money yet. We understood that you were heart and soul for Prince John, but if we have any more tales like this from you, your lands and goods will be confiscated, and you will be hanged, Master George."

"Leave everything to me," said George cheerfully, "I have a plan of operation, and if all goes well and I am sure that it will, I shall have all the money back and with good interest too. So do not worry for one moment more."

"See that you do," snarled the man, "for the Sheriff gets worse and worse bad tempered each day, and more unbearable. Soon I shall not be able to stand the man at all. So if you value your life and your property, get that money back, and make sure that none of it is missed ever again."

"Most interesting," said Robin Hood quietly.

"Why should you be so interested in the affairs of George-A-Green," said a voice close behind Robin, a voice that was far from being friendly, "we don't like snoopers round here, especially those who listen in when very private affairs are being discussed."

"I was not listening really," put in Robin quickly, "I was merely waiting to go inside to sell my cows to your master, and his voice was raised rather over much, I could not help hearing what he was saying, although I could not understand what he was talking about."

"You had better go inside now, and see what George-A-Green himself will think of you," snarled the man, pushing Robin inside the little stone built building.

The Sheriff's man turned round with a flushed face to see who was entering the small room, and then he snapped a few more sharp words to the man who was just leaving.

"You will get your money," he snapped, "now get out and keep out, I have a lot of work to do, and I shall never get through it all today, if you keep talking and talking. Now get out."

"Don't forget what I said," the departing stranger said, and he pushed past Robin without even so much as a glance.

"Who are you," said the man behind the table angrily, "and what are you doing here? You may go, Harry, and don't hang about listening outside. I am tired of you and your snooping ways. Be off with you, and the further you go, the better."

The man made a grimace and then made a quick exit, after giving Robin a searching glance, and that was the last that Robin saw of the man.

Then he turned to view George-A-Green.

Strangely he took an instant liking to the man, as much as he ever could take a liking to a man who professed to be on the side of the more and more hated Prince John.

George-A-Green suddenly reached out and pulled Robin's hood back off his face, stared at him for a few moments, and then a wide grin broke out on the man's heavy features.

"By all that's wonderful," he said quietly, "if it isn't Robin Hood himself."

The reception was not unfriendly, and Robin began to wonder more and more about the man and his supposed loyalties, for they had the air of being peculiarly divided.

"So you are the famous George-A-Green," said Robin, almost reaching out to shake the man's hand.

"I have been wanting to meet you for some time," said George-A-Green, staring at the figure before him as though he was observing a kind of a miracle.

Robin gave a half smile and asked quietly, "Why, Master George-A-Green, for what reason? To arrest me and turn me over to your friend, Prince John, or to change sides? What are your motives? But if you merely wish to take me prisoner, here I am all ready and waiting. Why are you hesitating, if that is your aim?"

"I have no ulterior motives," replied the giant of a man, "I have heard so much about this man Robin Hood, the man who has become a legend in his own time, and I am naturally vastly interested to meet you at long last. I suppose I could take you prisoner, but I candidly have no stomach for the job, and what it would lead up to, your hanging party. However, if you would care to fight for your freedom, good Robin, I would be delighted to battle with you with my stave. What say you, Outlaw Robin?"

"I have heard much of your stave work," said Robin, "and nothing would interest me more than to fight for my freedom. If you beat me in fair fight, I will give myself up without a struggle, but if you try any crooked tricks, you might find that I am not without friends around here."

"It shall be a fair fight," said George-A-Green, rising to his feet to tower above Robin by a good six inches.

"By the thunder," said Robin Hood, admiringly, "my man Little John would love a fight with you, you are just his type."

"Maybe he will have that pleasure before very long," said George-A-Green with a smile.

George-A-Green turned and led the way out of the hut and round the back where there was a quiet piece of flat ground that had not been churned up by the hooves of innumerable cattle.

Robin and George took their stands, having armed themselves with staves from the small collection of weapons leaned up against the rear of the small building, and then the fight began. For half an hour the battle swayed first one way and then the other, and the crack of weapons one against the other, brought a crowd of men from the field to watch, leaving the cows to graze in peace.

George fought like a man posessed of seven devils, but his great strength was no match for Robin's quickness and skill, and suddenly George's stave flew away into the air, and with a quick blow on to the top of George's head, Robin had his man down on the ground unconscious.

Robin leaned on his stave gasping for breath, to recover his strength after the long combat, whilst one of George's men poured a bucket of cold water over his master's head.

George-A-Green sat up spluttering and gasping, and his eyes were crossed for a few moments. Slowly, he began to recover his senses, and when his man had helped him to his feet, he said to Robin, "Well, sir, I think that you have earned your freedom, so be off with you and take those cows with you, if any of them be yours in truth. Go before I change my mind."

The men around glanced at George curiously, but they made no comments, and Robin made his quick departure, having first shaken the giant by the hand.

"Maybe we shall meet again soon," he said quietly, "what do you say?"

George rubbed his sore head with a grimace on his face, and then he said, "Be off with you, before I change my mind."

"Goodbye then," cried Robin, putting on once more the robes that he had discarded before the fight began. "I and my cows will be on our way. Goodbye, and thank you for an excellent fight."

He strode away to gather together his wandering cattle, keeping a sharp look-out for trouble. He had a deep-rooted feeling that he had been allowed to go a little too easily, and he wondered what sort of a trap the mysterious George was setting up for him.

As he walked about the field, he exchanged quick words with his own men, who told him that they had received his message and had pretended to be sick of the greenwood and their life there, and George had let them join his staff in such an easy-going way, that they could not quite reckon him up. Robin gave various instructions to the men, and then made his departure.

Robin walked his cows into the town of Wakefield, and by a lucky chance, was able to sell them for a good price to a farmer friend that he met on the bridge near the little chapel that stood so curiously in its centre. Robin then went inside the tiny building, and said a little prayer for King Richard.

The time seemed to go by on leaden feet, but at long last the darkness began to fall, and Robin emerged from a small wood at the roadside where he had spent his time sleeping and getting what rest he could in readiness for the long night of work that lay ahead of him.

It was pitch black night by the time Robin reached the trysting place where he had arranged to meet his men, and was surprised to find that they were already there waiting for him.

"It was far too easy, Robin," whispered Much, "the door of our sleeping quarters was locked on us presumably for the night, but a short while afterwards, somebody crept up to the door and unlocked it again, and even opened it to make sure that we would realise that the way was clear for us to go. Then when we went out into the corridor, there was not a soul about."

"It was quite spooky, actually," put in Red Rob of Batley, "the whole place seemed to be deserted. We had found out beforehand where the treasure was kept, and to our amazement, the door of the treasure house was unlocked too. Everything went too smoothly, everything was too unlocked and too unguarded. George-A-Green is up to something, and I'd like to know what it is. I don't like being so far from home; with all this treasure, somewhere along the way, there will be an ambush and we shall all be killed."

"Getting killed would not worry me," said Henry of Nottingham, "but I want this ransom money to get to the right source first, and the King freed and back in England and on the throne and ruling us again. Then I shall die very happily."

"The doors of the stables were unlocked too," said Red Rob, "and we were not hindered when we helped ourselves to as many pack horses and mules as we required. We got loaded up and away, although it was a nerve racking business. I prefer straight fights instead of all this mystery. When I get a knife in me, I want it in my chest, and not unexpectedly in my back."

"The best thing that we can do," said Robin, "is to get away from here as fast as possible and hasten back to Sherwood with this treasure trove. Twenty pack animals, all heavily laden, will travel slowly, but we shall have to do the best we can. I will send some of you ahead to scout out the way, the pack animals can go in the centre with a guard up each side, and I and the rest of the men will bring up the rear and fight whatever rear-guard actions are necessary. I only wish that there were far more of us in charge of this ransom."

"We were able to help ourselves to what weapons we required from the armoury," said Richard-A-Green, "the whole thing gets more and more mysterious as we go along. I simply cannot understand it."

"Let's get moving," said Robin, forming the men up into the order that he had in mind.

A few minutes later, the procession was making its way to the woods so that they could have as much cover as possible for their journey to Nottingham.

As they hurried over the bridge past the little chapel, Robin thought that he saw a shadow moving beside the building, and an arrow was placed in position in his bow with the speed of lightning.

Then the moon came out from behind a cloud, and Robin saw standing there un-armed and alone, the figure of George-A-Green. Then all went dark again, and when Robin could see clearly again in another wave of moonlight, George-A-Green had vanished as though he had been some kind of a ghost.

The journey back to Nottingham took quite a few days, and Robin hardly slept during that hair-raising trip, and all the time, he had the feeling that he was being followed. Every person that he met on the road made his heart beat a little faster, for he suspected that it was the beginning of a devastating ambush. Normally his work, although always being the type that kept him on the alert, was never quite so important as this particular mission, involving as it did, the life of the King of England.

He was thankful when he could get a message through to his base camp, asking for a good solid cover in case of attack. But before his own men could arrive on the scene to help him, the whole adventure was almost ruined and his plans put completely out of gear.

Chapter XIV

THE ATTACK AND A SURPRISE

HE had thought at first to split the treasure train into small groups, but on second thoughts, had decided that there was safety in numbers and therefore it would be best if the whole band of men and their precious charge stuck together in a solid band throughout the trip.

But the night before he could reasonably expect reinforcements, Robin was roused from his silent watch by the cracking of a twig. Instantly he was on the alert, and gave a signal to his men to arm themselves as quickly as possible.

Moments later, the woods seemed to be alive with soldiers, soldiers who wore the uniform of Prince John's soldiers.

The thought came into Robin's mind that he would die a thousand deaths before he would allow the treasure to fall into John's hands. He had felt all along that he and his men had been followed, but now he wondered why the attack had been held off for so long, if these were indeed the men who had been following along behind.

Then there was no more time for thought, only time for action.

He and his men fought like demons, and several of the Prince's soldiers never saw the light of another day as the results of the conflict. Five of Robin's men received severe injuries, and Robin himself was wounded in the left arm, but not seriously so. But all the same, the loss of so much blood took too much of his strength, and he felt more and more weak and dizzy as the battle proceeded.

With a determined effort, he fought off his faintness, but suddenly he realised that he and his small body of men were not going to win the fight, and help from his men was too far away to be of any use to him at this desperate moment.

The moonlight that came through the tree branches in fitful shafts of light, swirled before his eyes, and he almost wept as he realised that he could not go on with this battle much longer.

He had done his best but he was outnumbered, and as he took a quick glance at his men, he saw by their expressions, that they too were on the verge of being beaten down and killed by the great number of men who had attacked them.

A black mist swept before Robin's weary eyes, and then passed away again as he fought on, driven by some heaven-sent strength, but even that was failing him now and he sank to one knee as he fought off an adversary with his sword, a sword that was slippery and wet with blood. His left hand held a small dagger, but his hand was growing more and more stiff and useless, and the jabs that he did manage to get in with the small weapon were little better than useless.

He heard a shout from somewhere nearby, but thought that it was a cry of victory from his enemy. A scream of pain and terror failed to rouse him, and he imagined that one of his men had despatched one of the Prince's men in an extremely painful and lethal way.

Then suddenly the enemy turned their backs on the men of Sherwood, and found themselves face to face with a band of attackers who had suddenly come up behind them from amongst the trees.

Robin saw a great giant of a man wielding a broad sword with lethal effect, and thought that Little John had arrived with help.

Then before his dizzy eyes, swam the figure of a man that he had least expected to see.

The face was that of George-A-Green.

"I followed you, Robin," he cried, "because I thought that something like this might happen. I did not intend the treasure to fall into John's hands, or into the hands of the Sheriff either. But I will explain later."

"It's George-A-Green," cried Robin, and suddenly new strength flowed through his weary body, and he turned to dispose of four of John's men with slashing sword cuts. Then the woods were swarming with men dressed in George-A-Green's colours, and the weary men of John's army died fighting rather than go back to their master to be hanged for failing to get their hands on the treasure that was destined to be a King's ransom, although they did not know how the money was to be spent.

As suddenly as it had begun, the battle was over, and Robin and his weary men and their rescuers made their way farther into the forest, to get away from the scene of death that lay all around them. The few remaining adversaries dug graves for the fallen, and buried them, and then stole silently away into the night never to be seen again by their lord and master. The defeat had been too crushing for them to stomach.

Robin and the rest of the men washed the blood off themselves and bathed in the stream, and George-A-Green bound up their wounds as cleverly as any surgeon would have done.

Then they ate a meal that one of George's men had cooked for them, and Robin then ordered his men to lie down and rest and sleep if they could, whilst he helped to keep guard.

Robin was sitting there beneath a tree trying to keep his eyes open, and his ears open for another snapping of a tell-tale twig, when George-A-Green came and sat down beside him.

"I dare say that you are wondering what I am up to," said George quietly, "but now that I can speak freely, I will tell you candidly that I am absolutely sick and tired being taxed and robbed by Prince John's men. Our own Sheriff in Yorkshire is every bit as bad as your man, and I pay enormous taxes to him. I have to pay such a vast rent for my farm, that I am being financially ruined. But I have got my own back at last."

"How," asked Robin, hanging on to every word that the man spoke.

"I am for Richard and always have been," said George-A-Green, "and when your men turned up as prisoners and said they were tired of life in the greenwood, I guessed that this was the very opposite to the truth. Then when I recognised you, I guessed that you were after the treasure that had been brought through the forest under your very nose, amongst the people who were going to the market day festivities. You must have boiled over when you saw it going by, and could do nothing to get it, Robin."

"I could have burst with rage," said Robin, scowling at the bitter memory.

"The Sheriff of York is supposed to be coming to see me this coming morning," went on George-A-Green, "and is going to take away all the treasure that I am supposed to have collected and hoarded for Prince John, and because of a disagreement I had with him a while ago about storing the Sheriff of Nottingham's treasure in my vaults, he is going to confiscate my furniture and my treasure and my cattle. But when he arrives, he will find that this particular bird has flown. I let you take the treasure away, and then I followed you at a distance, in case our two Sheriffs and their men to get it back again. I sold my cattle and my furniture last week, so he will have an empty farm house on his hands. I didn't even plant any grain for crops this year, so he will have empty fields as well."

Robin shook with laughter, and felt the strength returning to him almost in leaps and bounds.

"It was a good thing that you did follow with your men, and I thank you for all that you have done," said Robin brightly, "I have never been so near to being defeated ever in my life before. If it had not been for your timely help, we should all have been dead, and the treasure in the vaults of Nottingham Castle."

"By the way," asked George-A-Green, "why did you come so far and go to such great lengths to get this vast treasure, for there is a very great deal of money there. What do you need so much money for so urgently? I have heard tell that you have intensified your efforts in Sherwood forest also, so collect wealth. Why?"

Robin gave a secret smile.

"There is indeed a great deal of money there," he said quietly, "a King's ransom, in fact. That is exactly what it is for, the King's ransom."

"So Richard is alive and a prisoner," gasped George-A-Green," "our Richard. Where is he? Is he well?"

"The Archduke of Austria took him prisoner," said Robin, "a base piece of treachery against a man who fought beside him in the Holy Wars. Now he is demanding this ransom, or Richard will be killed inside of the year. We had not a great deal of time to collect such a large sum of money, and get it transported to Austria. I only hope that the Archduke does not put up his price, when he receives the treasure. I will tell you more later, but now my brain reels with weariness, and I cannot think clearly any more tonight. But thank you once again, good Master George, for saving us all, and for saving the King's ransom and the King himself."

So saying, Robin's head lolled forward, and he went off into a deep sleep, and did not wake again until the sun was high in the sky.

Chapter XV

BLONDEL AGAIN

A week later whilst Robin Hood was swearing in George-A-Green and his men into the band of men in Lincoln Green, the sound of a whistle blown three times sounded through the wood, and a look of expectant joy passed over Robin's face. He quickly finished off the little swearing in ceremony, and then hurried off into the woods with his greatest friend Will Scarlet at his side.

At the pre-arranged place, they found Blondel with a large body of soldiers on horse-back, and a train of pack horses heavily laden with bags of gold that had been donated by the various Barons who were only too anxious to see Richard once more on the throne of England, and the treacherous Prince John put well and firmly in his place.

Robin escorted Blondel back to camp, together with his men, and the treasure that they had brought with them, and when they had been fed and rested, plans were made to take the King's ransom over the channel to France and through to Austria. The trip would be long and hazardous, but a strong force of fighting men should be able to deal with any enemy that might come their way. Richard had many friends in France also, who would be only too willing to help him and his men.

George-A-Green sent most of his men, and Robin let three hundred of his own men go to escort the King back to England. The Archduke would not dare to put up his price in the face of such a large fighting force, backing up the loyal men that Blondel had with him, and those who were waiting on both sides of the channel to do their turn of duty.

A large ship fully manned had been waiting impatiently at Dover for weeks now, ready to take its part in the rescue operation, and Robin glowed with pride as he pictured the welcome that the King would receive when he once more returned to the shores of England.

But he little knew what dangers and adventures would really be waiting for the King on his return, and what a vital part he himself was to play before England was to be once more a free and glorious country.

The night before Blondel was due to set out on his journey, Robin and his wife Marion staged the greatest banquet that Sherwood had ever seen, and the festivities went on until the first light of dawn streaked across the sky.

Then Blondel rested a while, and after that, he and his men set forth on their dangerous journey.

As they progressed towards the South East coast, they gathered together more and more fighting men, and by the time they saw the English Channel spreading greyly before them, they were in great heart, and went aboard the waiting ship joyfully.

They received a send-off that was heart warming to put it mildly, for almost the entire population of the little town had turned out to watch the ship depart, for news had got out that the ship was going to fetch Richard home again.

The Sheriff of the County of Kent sat gnawing his knuckles in his room at the castle, helpless in the face of such opposition to do anything to stop them.

After all, he could not arrest a whole town full of people, who also seemed to have the backing of his entire fighting force.

He sat alone ... and helpless.

Chapter XVI

THE END OF AN ENEMY

ROBIN HOOD stared about him keenly, his ears straining to pick up the sound of a snapping twig or the neigh of a strange horse. His eyes flashed at the quick flutter of a bird as it shot out of the trees and down on to the sun-dappled grass, and he located the thing that might just as easily have been the arrow of an enemy, or the quick leap from a hidden foe on to his back.

Several times recently, spies had been caught by the men of Sherwood, spies who had come in many forms from old women and witches, to weary travellers who had turned out to be far from weary when they had been caught, travellers who had come from no farther away than Nottingham. Men who had the appearance of innocent travellers and friends of King Richard, had given themselves away through some mistake of speech, and had been shown up as friends of Prince John. Monks had been found to be wearing chain mail under their robes, and messages and money for John in their saddle bags.

Even damsels in distress had turned out to be friends of John, by the careless wearing of some emblem or other that gave them away.

It was becoming more and more difficult to sort out the wheat from the chaff amongst the travellers through Sherwood Forest, and it was more and more difficult to find men who were genuinely fit to be members of the band of men in Lincoln Green.

Traitors were ten a penny, and Robin began to pray for the day when King Richard would return to England and proclaim himself the rightful King once more.

Surely that day could not be far away.

The disposal of the spies was not too hard a task, for most of them put up such a battle when cornered, that they were killed in the resulting fights.

But at the back of his mind, Robin had the feeling that Prince John was planning an all-out offensive against his enemies, to get himself into an extremely firm position before his brother Richard returned to England and claimed the throne. The men of Sherwood would doubtless be near the top of the list of people that John wished to have disposed of before the day of Richard's return came along.

One morning as Robin and Will Scarlet were returning from a little encounter with an extremely rich Baron on a by-path in the forest, and they were smiling at the sight of the heavily laden pack mule that they had persuaded the Baron to part with. The smiles were to be wiped off their faces suddenly and tragically, and things were never to be quite the same for Robin, ever again.

The two friends entered a forest glade with a light step, to draw to a sudden horror-stricken halt.

The grass was soaked in blood, and six of Robin's men lay dead with arrows in their backs.

"Some of our men," gasped Robin, "six of them. Judging by the arrows in their backs, and the fact that they had obviously not had time to fit arrows to their bows or draw their swords, they were taken completely by surprise. Oh, this is dreadful."

"Be careful," said Will Scarlet, "the attackers may still be about."

Robin seized his horn and blew a mighty blast upon it, a blast that echoed from end to end of the forest, and the sound was heard even as far away as Nottingham.

The Sheriff paused in his stride and a thin smile twisted his lips, as he imagined Robin Hood in a state of dire distress. He rubbed his hands together and wondered how successful this new little scheme of his was going to be. Some day he would get the better of the outlaw, and he hoped that this would be that particularly hoped for day.

In Sherwood Forest, the woods became alive with men, for although Robin had sent a goodly number of men to escort his beloved King back to England, the forests were still swarming with a large army of men in Lincoln Green, and a large fighting force could be raised almost at a moment's notice.

Robin and Will fitted arrows to their bows, and stared up into the tree-tops and around them into the woods, but the enemy must have flown. There was not a sighting of a soldier.

Robin and Will then hurried over to their dead companions, and looked into the dead faces of the men that they had so greatly admired and depended upon for help, and their eyes were filled with anger at the outrage.

Robin was just turning to speak to Will Scarlet, when there came the sudden hiss of an arrow shot from the trees above them, and Will Scarlet slumped forward with an arrow in his back, an arrow that went so deep that its head came through his chest. He gave a dull cough and fell forward, dead.

A cry of agony broke from Robin's lips as he saw his friend die so suddenly, and then in a flash, he fired an arrow up into the branches above him, a random arrow that did not find a mark.

"Come down, whoever you are," he shouted, "come down and fight like a man. Come down, or I will go on shooting until you fall dead."

A sudden activity amongst the tree branches heralded the arrival of the man who had evidently shot the fatal arrow at Will Scarlet, and then the man was on the ground and drawing his sword.

"It was worth risking death from your men's arrows, Robin," said the man, "just to have the pleasure of getting close enough to you to fight you to the death. I want nothing more out of life than to put my sword through you. I have been dreaming of this moment for years."

"You won't get away with my death," cried Robin, "for if you do succeed in killing me, you will be instantly filled with my men's arrows. Now take off that mask and that great hat and cape, and let me see who killed my greatest friend. If you dare look me in the face now."

"Don't you recognise me, Robert Fitzooth," shouted the man, flicking his sword at Robin's face, "I am Guy of Gisborne. This is the last round, Robin. When I have killed you, I have to blow six blasts on that horn of yours, and the sound will tell the Sheriff that you are dead. Of course, if you yield now, your men may be spared, and only you will be hanged."

"You would not live to blow one blast, never mind six," shouted Robin in a fury of rage.

He flicked out his sword and whipped off the mask that hid the man's face with the sharp point of his weapon, revealing the face of Guy of Gisborne, the man that he now hated more than any man on earth, including the Sheriff and Prince John.

Guy flung off the remainder of his disguising clothes, and waited until some of Robin's men had tenderly gathered up Will Scarlet's body and laid it under the trees at the side of the clearing beside the bodies of the six men of Sherwood who had been so treacherously murdered.

Robin watched with smouldering eyes, and then turned to face his enemy.

Robin and Guy faced each other, swords in hand, and the sun glinting against the metal. Then the fight began.

It was a hard fight, and for an incredibly long time, the forest glade rang with the clash of steel. Suddenly Guy drew his dagger and threw it straight at Robin's throat, but Robin was a second too quick for it, and the knife whistled past him scratching the skin as it went, to bury itself deep in a tree bole. The men of Sherwood watched with bated breath, and bows and arrows at the ready, for Guy would not live an instant if he killed Robin Hood.

Robin drew his dagger and flung it at Guy, but the metal clanked against the man's breast, and Robin realised that Guy was wearing chain mail under his tunic. He changed his tactics instantly, and flicked off the steel helmet that Guy was wearing, and then he raised his sword high above his head in both hands and sliced downwards on to the unprotected brown haired head. Guy gave a scream of agony, and then sank down on to the grass to die slowly and painfully.

Robin marched over to his fallen foe and struck the head off the dead shoulders with one sweep of his sword, and then taking off his own cape, he wrapped the severed head up in its folds.

It was at this moment that one of his men called out to him, "Robin, the Sheriff's men have taken Little John prisoner, and at this very moment, they are taking him in chains to Nottingham Castle."

Robin glanced coldly down at Guy's headless body, and then he stripped off its clothes. Taking off his own clothes and passing them to one of his own men, to take to camp, he dressed quickly in the dead man's garments and armour, and covered his face with the discarded mask. After doing this, he took a deep breath and blew six blasts on his horn, and turned to walk off in the direction of Nottingham without a word to his men.

The Sheriff heard the six blasts on the horn, and screamed out in unholy joy, "Robin Hood is dead, Guy has killed him. The outlaw is dead."

Then he marched up and down his room, his fists clenched up beneath his chin, muttering animal sounds of jubilation.

A while later, the hooded and cloaked figure of the man that he imagined to be Guy of Gisborne, was shown in through the door, and the Sheriff rushed to embrace him. He was so excited, that he did not notice that his greetings and embrace were not returned.

"Guy," screamed the Sheriff, "you have killed him. The enemy is dead. Oh, this is a great day for Prince John. I will give you anything that you want in return for this great service. What do you want, friend?"

Robin imitated Guy's voice as he said, "I want very little reward, his death is enough of a reward to me. I have always hated the man, and he is best where he is, burning his soul out in Hades. I have his head here in this bundle, but please do not uncover it until I have made my departure, for I have seen enough blood for one day. I want to see no more of it for a long time, I am sickened with the sight of it. But there is just one thing I do want, Sheriff."

"What is it," fussed the Sheriff, his eyes fixed gloatingly on the blood-stained green cloaked bundle on the table, "I will give you everything that you ask for, that is a promise."

"I have killed the man," said Robin, "now give me Little John."

The Sheriff shouted out to his scribe who was working in an adjoining room, "Scribe, order the soldiers to bring Little John here to this room."

The scribe hurried away to do his bidding, and the Sheriff began to stride up and down the room, almost insane with joy.

Robin Hood walked to a window and opened it wide, as though the very smell of the Sheriff and everything in his room stank so much that he could not bear it.

Minutes elapsed and then the door was flung open, and Little John was forced into the room by a body of soldiers. He glared at the Sheriff, and put up such a fight, that he almost broke free, and would indeed have done so had not Robin Hood gone up to him to pretend to help the soldiers.

Robin whispered in his ear, "Steady, John, I have come to take you away."

Little John pretended to struggle for a while longer, and then he said, "All right, I surrender to this man. Take me away and kill me, whoever you may be."

"Kill him," shouted the Sheriff, "kill him, and bring his head back to me."

"I will be back soon, Sheriff," said Robin, "when I have dealt with this scoundrel."

With a knife prodding into Little John's back, Robin marched him out of the room and down the great staircase and out of the castle. Across the courtyard the two men marched, and then through the streets of Nottingham, and out of the city to the forest.

They marched along for two miles, and then Robin said, "We will relax now, John. I see our own men up in the trees waiting for any of the Sheriff's men that dare still set foot in the forest on this black day."

"What is black about it," asked Little John quickly, "what has gone wrong?"

Robin told him what had happened, his face white and his eyes blazing with anger, and then his voice broke as he finished the tragic story.

Little John stared at Robin in horror, and then Robin tore off the cloak and mask and steel helmet and tunic and chain mail vest, ad threw them into a pond that was situated at the side of the pathway.

Then he threw off the rest of his clothes and dived into the pond as though he wanted to wash off the blood and also the feeling of personal contact with the clothes of his most hated enemy. Little John stood watching him from the bank, his eyes bleak, stricken with grief at the news of Will Scarlet's death.

After a while, Robin crawled out of the water and dried himself on John's cloak, before putting on the breeches again.

Then the two men turned and walked away towards the camp.

The first signs of impending danger were heralded by the neigh of a horse in the distance, and Robin drew his sword so quickly that it was like a flash of lightning in his hands. The thunder of hooves grew steadily nearer, and then suddenly twelve of the Sheriff's men rode upon them.

The fight that followed was deadly and un-equal, but Robin and John killed four of the Sheriff's men in the first five minutes of the fight. They were turning to despatch the remainder, when the thunder of hooves came to their ears, and a few moments later, a Knight clad in black armour roared up the path, his sword already drawn.

The battle that followed was brief but blood-stained, and soon the Sheriff's men lay dead or dying on the reddened grass, and Robin and John stood leaning on their slippery swords to regain their breath.

Then Robin turned to thank the man who had come to their aid in such a crucial moment, but he had not waited to have words with them. They barely had time to catch a glimpse of him as he raced away along the path in hot pursuit of the last remaining soldiers, and then he was gone from their sight. The two remaining soldiers would be easy meat for his sword.

Robin and John cleaned their swords, and gathered up the swords and daggers of the slain and wounded, and then without a backward glance, made their way back to camp.

"A knight in black armour," mused Robin, "I wonder who he was? Who do you think he was, John?"

Little John paused in his tracks, and a smile broke out on his face.

"I hardly dare guess," he said, "but I can only hope and pray that it was . . ."

He did not end his sentence.

The two men glanced at each other, and then Robin said, "That would be too much to hope for. But let us pray that it was, all the same."

The Sheriff had watched his guests make their departure, and had been so overcome with joy at the death of Robin Hood, that he forgot all about the bundle on the table.

He called to his scribe and told him the news, and ordered him to spread the news all over Nottingham, and also ordered that great festivities be staged for the population.

The scribe shrugged his shoulders and said remotely, "I hardly dare say this, but I have the feeling that there will not be much celebrating in Nottingham over the death of Robin Hood. He had many friends here. They will grieve at his passing. He will be a sad loss to them."

The Sheriff glared at him in speechless rage for a few moments, and then he strode to the table and began to unwrap the dreadful bundle that lay there.

"Let Robin Hood's head be stuck on a spear and displayed in the centre of the market square," he shouted. Seizing a spear that lay at the far end of the great long table, he returned to the bundle to impale it himself.

He completed the unwrapping of the bundle, and stared in sickened distaste at the back of the head that lay there. With the point of the spear, he turned the head over so that he could see the face.

A moment later, his scream echoed through the castle, a scream that was followed by more and more screams whilst his soldiers and members of his staff rushed to his room to see what was the matter.

"Robin Hood is not dead," the Sheriff gurgled, "the head is that of Guy of Gisborne. So who was the man who brought me this thing? Who was he? He took Little John away with him too. I let them walk away from here unhindered. It was Robin Hood himself. Robin Hood, and I let him go."

Suddenly the Sheriff's knees sagged, and he grasped at the cloak on which lay the head of Guy of Gisborne. Foaming at the mouth, he fell in a fit, dragging the cloak on top of him.

The head of Guy of Gisborne fell to the floor with a thud.

Seconds later, the Sheriff was dead.

Chapter XVII

THE TOURNAMENT

IT will be a dangerous trip for you, Robin," said Little John, eyeing his friend anxiously, "to go right in to the centre of Ashby-De-La-Zouche for the Grand Tournament. Prince John will be there with all his friends and followers around him, in full force. You will be in the centre of them all, alone and a great way from home. I wish you would take a covering of men with you."

Robin gave a hearty laugh and clapped his friend on his broad back with a thump from his powerful hand.

"Little John, you old woman," cried Robin, "I am going alone. Prince John would never dare to have a finger laid on me at such an event. He is trying to push himself forward as King of England, but he has too many enemies all over the country now. He would not dare to do such an unpopular thing as have Robin Hood arrested publicly at such a gathering."

"I'm not so sure," put in Little John, "but if you want to go and go alone, you will do so. Nothing any of us can do or say, will stop you."

Little John looked keenly once more at his friend, and a feeling of relief crept through him, for this was the first time since the death of Will Scarlet, that Robin had lost that bleak-eyed and heartbroken look from his face. Robin was once more beginning to show interest in the affairs of this world, and Little John was whole-heartedly delighted at the change in the man.

Robin outlined his plans to Little John, and then went to tell his wife Marion what had been decided.

That night, a small band of Robin's men returned to the camp after their trip abroad to escort King Richard home to England, and Robin and his principal men were the first to hear the news that they brought.

"King Richard is back in England," said the Captain of the band, "and so are the rest of our men, all safe and well. We paid the ransom money and retrieved our King, and escorted him to the coast and on to a boat without too much trouble. But when we got to Dover, he inisted on slipping into the country unnoticed, and away on his own devices, with only a small body of men to guard him. He said he would proclaim himself when he was ready to do so."

Little John roared with laughter, almost too delighted at the news to speak, and then he said, "So Richard wants to go his own way, however dangerous his chosen course may be. Robin and Richard make a fine pair, sticking their necks out into any danger that threatens, rather than do things the safe way."

Friar Tuck chuckled plumply and remarked, "They will never learn, either of them, except the hard way. Even then I doubt if they will learn."

The captain gave full details of the rescue operations, and all that had followed, and then he turned to receive a further band of men who were just straggling in from the outer forest.

All that night, they returned in small batches under the cover of darkness, so that they would not inadvertantly give away the location of this most secret of all Robin Hood's secret hiding places in the forest.

The following morning, Robin donned his new suit of Lincoln Green, armed himself with his newly cleaned sword and dagger, and his bow and a good supply of arrows, and then set off on his horse for Ashby-De-La-Zouche, to the tournaments. Marion kissed him and bade him farewell, and stood watching him ride along the path until he was out of sight. She breathed a little prayer for him, as she watched him make his departure. Then she turned with a sigh and went back to the various tasks that always kept her fully occupied in the forest.

The tending of the sick and wounded was an important part of her work, then she helped with the making of clothes, and general supervision of the domestic side of the running of the camp. She never had a moment to spare, from cooking meals at various odd times of the night or day, to the binding of feathers on to the arrows to act as flights. No matter what the season of the year, she was always busy.

In due course, Robin reached Ashby-De-La-Zouche and put up at a small inn near the outskirts of the town, in case he had to make a quick getaway at a moment's notice, and then he rode to the fields of sport.

He watched the jousting and regretted that entry was reserved for the Knights of the land, and at that moment, Robin could not qualify for the events as his title had been confiscated. He stood beside his horse watching the first event on the programme, wondering who the unknown knight was who was so obviously defeating all who came up against him. When the last opponent had been defeated, Prince John presented the prize grudgingly.

The next event was a mock battle, and once more the unknown knight was well in evidence, and led his men in a brave display of horsemanship and swordsmanship and when it came to the lancing of an enemy off a horse, he was second to none.

The unknown knight looked like winning this event also, but his opponent, who was Sir Brian de Bois-Guilbert, a Norman baron, began to lose what temper he had left, and deliberately tripped up the horse that bore the unknown knight, and sent him sprawling to the ground under the flailing hooves of the horse that had borne him so bravely throughout the mock battle.

Sir Brian raised his lance as though he would kill the man on the ground, but at that crucial moment, a knight in black armour thundered on to the field and cried out in a ringing voice, "I will fight you for your victim, Sir Knight. If you win, you can kill him if you must. If I win, he is my man for life and can thus serve me."

A great hush settled on the crowds that surrounded the field of combat, and there was much speculation as to the identity of the strange knight in his fantastic black armour.

Robin Hood watched the two men dismount, and his heart beat faster as he watched the sword battle that followed. Only one man in the world could fight like that, and Robin's heart warmed and his pulses quickened at the thoughts that were passing through his mind as the fight proceeded.

The crowd grew wild with delight as they watched the two men in armour, and listened to the clash of swords. Suddenly it was all over. The Black Knight flicked the sword out of the hand of Sir Brian, flicked up the vizor of his steel helmet with the tip of his sword, and then made as though to thrust the weapon straight through the right eye of the Norman baron.

"I give," cried the Baron, his voice high-pitched through exhaustion and defeated pride.

The cheers that rose from the crowds of spectators were almost deafening, and when the Black Knight went and raised the vizor of the unknown knight who had been standing waiting by the Royal box, it was revealed that the young knight was none other than Sir Wilfred of Ivanhoe. The excitement and cheering grew to an almost unbearable pitch.

The Black Knight walked over to the Royal Box and took the trophy from the reluctant hands of Prince John and turned and presented it to Sir Wilfred, and then the two men mounted their horses and rode out of the field with their own men close at their heels.

Sir Wilfred was known to be a great man for King Richard, and feelings had run so high during the sword battle and its surprising revelation at the end of it, that it would not have been surprising if some of Prince John's supporters had retaliated against the victors.

The following day, the archery contests took place.

Thirty yeomen presented themselves, and amongst them was Robin Hood clad in his new green suit.

Prince John scowled at Robin through narrowed eyelids and snarled, "Who is that fellow?"

The Provost of the Lists glanced at the parchment roll in his hand and said, "It says here that his name is Locksley. Robert Locksley, Sire."

"I thought so," cried John, a triumphant note sounding in his voice, "I thought so."

He stared at Robin Hood, and the eyes of the two men met with hatred burning in them. Prince John rose to his feet, and was about to order the arrest of his enemy, when a hand was laid restrainingly on his.

"Not here, Your Highness," said a quiet over-smooth voice, "not here. Just wait until a little later, when a good opportunity will arise."

Prince John turned to stare into the eyes of the new Sheriff of Nottingham, and he saw the glitter in the cold black eyes, and also saw the thin smile on the evil lips.

He re-seated himself and his raised hand fell to rest upon his knees, to clutch at the cloth of his coat viciously. Then he pulled himself together, and signalled for the archery contest to commence.

One after the other the contestants tried their skill with bow and arrow, and the weakest of them were quickly eliminated. So the morning wore on. It was almost noon by the time Robin Hood and Hubert of Nottingham, who was one of Prince John's most ardent supporters, were left alone to fight it out between them.

Each man had two shots at the target, and the prize was to be a small bugle horn filled with silver coins.

Hubert aimed carefully at the target, and drawing his bow, shot an arrow that went dead in to the centre of the bulls eye, and his second shot landed a fraction of an inch away from it.

Hubert's supporters cheered until they were hoarse, thinking that Hubert had won. But Robin took his stand and the supporters jeered him, thinking that he was wasting his time.

Hubert had aimed carefully, taking a long time over each shot, but Robin shot his first arrow with scarcely a glance. The arrow sped through the air in a high arc, and landed on the bulls eye, knocking one of Hubert's arrows from the target board. A cheer rang out from the spectators, and they all rose to their feet trying to get a better view of the amazing contest. Robin slowly choose another arrow and fitted it to his bow. The arrow flashed through the air, and landed on the remaining arrow that Hubert had shot on to the bulls eye. Hubert's arrow was split from end to end, and Robin's arrow landed on the bulls eye, sending the broken arrow flying in splinters in all directions.

The crowd screamed its excitement, and Hubert raised both fists to the skies, shouting out, "It is a draw. I have not been beaten."

"It could not be a fairer win for Locksley," came a great voice from the crowd, "Locksley is the winner."

There were cries of "No, never," from Hubert's supporters, but Robin raised his hands and asked to be allowed to speak.

"I will challenge Hubert of Nottingham to a deciding contest," shouted Robin.

Whereupon Robin fetched a willow wand that was a good six feet long, and peeled it. Then he drove it into the ground and retreated one hundred yards.

"You have the first shot, good Hubert," said Robin politely.

Hubert glared at him shouting, "This is impossible. Nobody could hit such a target."

He fitted an arrow to his bow and shot it at the wand. The arrow made the wand twitch, but went on to land a yard farther along the path of flight.

Robin fitted his arrow, and with scarcely a glance, he shot his arrow and a great gasp went up from the crowd as Robin's arrow pinned the willow wand in an arch to the ground.

"The winner," shouted the crowd in unison, and then a great cheer broke out.

Robin made his way to the Royal Box, and bowed low and mockingly as Prince John presented the prize to him, and made as though to shake his hand. Robin touched the Prince's fingers, and then wiped the tips of his fingers on his tunic as though he had touched something slimy and unclean.

Prince John gritted his teeth together in a rage and broke a back tooth as a result. His eyes blazed with fury.

Robin gave a low bow and withdrew from the field, carrying his prize in his hands.

Sir Brian de Bois-Guilbert whispered into Prince John's ear, "Shall I follow and take Locksley prisoner, Your Highness?"

Prince John was trembling with rage, his eyes cold and hard, and he nodded his head sharply in assent.

As the next event was commencing, Sir Brian rode out of the field, and away along the winding narrow streets of the town.

Robin had got a good start, and was well away into the woods before Sir Brian caught up with him. Robin drew his horse to the side of the path when he heard the thunder of hooves coming after him in obvious pursuit, and drew his sword.

"Robin Hood," cried the horseman, as he rode into sight, "I arrest you in the King's name."

"Where is your warrant," cried Robin Hood, "the warrant with the King's signature and seal upon it?"

"It is waiting back in Ashby-De-La-Zouche," replied Sir Brian, furious at Robin's calmness and coolness.

"Did the King sign it in Ashby this morning," asked Robin calmly.

"The King is signing it at this very moment," shouted Sir Brian, blustering and growing red in the face with anger.

"Is Richard already in Ashby," asked Robin, his eyes snapping with dislike at this bullying Norman baron.

"I did not say Richard," shouted Sir Brian, "I said the King."

"That is right, the King," said Robin with a smile, "King Richard. Is he already in Ashby?"

Sir Brian choked with fury.

"When you show me a warrant with King Richard's name and signature upon it," said Robin coldly, "you may arrest me ... in the King's name."

Sir Brian whipped out his sword, and made as though to charge straight at Robin Hood and bring him crashing down off his horse.

"Not so fast, Sir Knight," said Robin Hood, "I am more interested in your strength of arm, rather than the strength of your sword. How about dismounting, and fighting me without sword or dagger or bow and arrow? What say you, Sir Knight?"

"I can defeat you in any manner that you wish, Yeoman," snarled the Baron, dismounting and throwing aside his arms. He had discarded his bulky armour at the Tournament fields, but was still wearing his chain mail vest.

Robin pointed to it and smiled, then he said, "Do you wear your chain mail vest to prevent yourself from getting bruised in a fall, Baron?"

Sir Brian pulled off his chain mail vest with an effort, and then took off his under garment, and then he turned to face Robin Hood, wearing only his breeches and shoes and stockings. Robin was soon similarly stripped.

They tied their horses to a tree branch, and then adjourned to a clearing, and circled round each other with hands at the ready.

Then the fight began.

"Three falls for a win," shouted Robin, as he seized his adversary round the waist and raised him up off his feet to hold him up on his shoulders to spin him round a dozen times before flinging the man down on to the ground with a crash that knocked the breath out of the baron's body.

Sir Brian gasped and lay shaken to the marrow for a few moments, and then he rose to his feet and grasped Robin round the waist, trying to crush the breath out of his body for ever, but Robin began to spin round on his feet again, until Sir Brian came in violent contact with a tree bole and released his hold, to go rolling breathlessly along the ground, and into a muddy pool of water.

Cursing, the great man struggled to his feet once more, and made a dive at Robin that would have sent him crashing to the ground in a back breaking fall if the hold could have been made. But Robin stepped quickly aside, and Sir Brian, out of control now, crashed head first into a tree, and into a pit of black unconsciousness. He was completely unconscious when Robin heaved him up on to his horse, and tied him in position, and then Robin tied the bundle of clothing on the rear of the horse. Then he turned the horse round, and whipped it off so that it would race back to Ashby-De-La-Zouche as fast as its legs could carry it.

A little while afterwards, in the middle of an important event at the tournaments, the horse rode into the centre of the field to the consternation of all present, and Prince John thought for a few exhilarating moments that Robin was being delivered to him in this extraordinary manner.

When Prince John saw who the victim really was, he gave a shout of rage that resounded all round the field.

John's supporters were horrified when they saw who the unconscious man was, but the friends of Richard, and there were many of them at Ashby-De-La-Zouche that day, smothered their laughter behind their hands and held in their mirth until they were in the safety of their own homes.

There they laughed until they ached too much to laugh any more.

Prince John never lived the matter down as far as the citizens of Ashby were concerned.

The men of Sherwood were to chuckle for months, at the thought of what had happened in the woods after the Tournament.

But Prince John grew more and more determined to come to final grips with Robin Hood as soon as possible, and to win. The affair of the tournament was to have extremely serious consequences for Robin in the distant future.

Chapter XVIII

A PROCLAMATION AND A SURPRISE

THE new Sheriff of Nottingham stood in the centre of his office at Nottingham Castle, a sneer twisting his lips, his eys black and hard as jet, and the expression on his face registering complete disapproval of the fittings and the general set out of the apartment.

He walked briskly to the window and stared out at the town below, and the farther aspect of Sherwood Forest.

Somewhere amongst those trees lived Robin Hood and his gang of outlaws, and the new Sheriff wondered why his late uncle, the old Sheriff, had found it so impossible to catch the outlaw chief and his men after all those years in office. The man must have been simple-minded to allow a mere band of uneducated brigands to get the better of him so often and so thoroughly. The Sheriff had even got killed by what the new man considered to be a very transparent trick.

The young Sheriff gave a snort of disgust and rang a hand bell that stood on his desk.

The door the outer office opened moments later, and the Sheriff turned quickly and shouted to the scribe, "For Heavens sake, man, get this place cleaned up and some of those rubbishy papers dealt with or thrown away. Go through everything and get all the outstanding business attended to immediately. My uncle must have spent his years in office in sleeping on the job."

"I will see to it all at once, sire," said the scribe, briskly gathering up an armful of papers at random and hurrying from the room before the new Sheriff could begin to make any of his searing remarks to him. The scribe had taken as much as he could stand from the Sheriff earlier on in the morning. Any more cutting remarks, and the man felt that he would run away and join Robin Hood in the forest of Sherwood. Surely Robin could do with a man to write his letters for him, and keep his books. That was, if outlaws did keep account books.

The old Sheriff had been an overpowering bully, but this new man was cold and vicious and so cunning, that nobody knew what he would get up to next. Nobody was safe whilst he was at work in the castle, or anywhere else for that matter.

Some day somebody would drive a knife into that scheming heart, if the Sheriff did not stop playing his mean little tricks to trap his staff into making false statements and getting themselves punished for things that they had not done.

The old Sheriff had bullied and sworn and ordered men to be whipped without reason, and then gone to watch the performance of the punishment. But this new man spoke very little and could cold-bloodedly order a hanging with a smile on his lips, and ice in his eyes. When he did speak, the staff turned sick with fear.

This nephew of the late Sheriff was quickly growing to be one of the most hated men in the county, and he seemed to even revel in the fact.

The Sheriff picked up a letter that lay on a small table at his side, and read the contents with smouldering eyes. The letter was from a friend of his in the south country, and it warned him that King Richard had returned to England, and was not to be found anywhere. He had gone into a hiding place the moment he had set foot on Dover's soil, and nobody knew where that hiding place was. It was essential now at this moment and without any delay, to announce to the people of England that Richard was dead, and to proclaim that Prince John was now the King. When Richard did eventually choose to make his appearance in public, he could be hailed as an imposter, a man so like Richard in appearance that he had the gall to proclaim himself King and claim the throne of England for himself.

Prince John arrived in Nottingham that afternoon and drove straight to the castle, and was taken without delay to the Sheriff's office.

After the first exchange of greetings, the Sheriff showed him the letter that was troubling him so much.

Prince John read the message with glittering eyes, and then ordered the Town Crier to go out and summons the entire population to the market place that evening, when he himself would make a vastly important speech to them.

Then he turned to the Sheriff and said, "I too have heard that my brother has returned to England, but I have been unable to find out where he is living. He has so many friends, unfortunately, that he could be hiding in any of a hundred different great houses. If only he would show himself, we could deal with him in a decisive way, but the man is cunning, and is playing a cat and mouse game with us. It almost seems that he is waiting for us to show our hands, also."

Prince John ate a large meal with quiet concentration, and then made his way to the market square, heavily guarded but with a great show of banners and pomp and circumstance. It was the best show that the Sheriff could put on for him, at such short notice.

The crowds that lined the streets were quiet and subdued, and when the Prince reached the crowded market square and climbed up on to the platform that had been specially erected for the occasion, only his own followers raised a voice to cheer him. There were more sullen faces than joyous ones, and John noticed this fact with cold fury. Someday he would make the people of Nottingham go down on their knees to him, but he had more vital things on his mind at this moment, than the crushing of the population of Nottingham.

He made his speech telling the people of Nottingham that King Richard was dead, and that he would be proclaiming himself as their King in the very near future now. He waited for the cheers that he was sure would come now, but the response was chilling to put it mildly. A good deal of cheering was heard, but it was not the great roar of approval that he had expected, and he scowled blackly as he stared down at the mass of upturned faces.

Somebody had once told him that he could not arrest and punish the entire population of a town, and now the full force of this meaning was made clear to him, it would be impossible to put them all in to prison, or even to start to punish them separately. The whole town would have to be made to groan under his heel, but even Prince John knew that such a course would create too many enemies for him and for his cause.

Suddenly John's keen eyes picked out the figure of a woman near the platform, and his pulses quickened as he recognised her. It was Marion, the wife of Robin Hood, with two companions. He recognised Lorna the wife of Allan-A-Dale, and also Betriss, the wife of George-A-Green. He almost choked with excitement.

Prince John whispered something into the Sheriff's ear, and the man nodded in assent, and then turned to order that the horses be taken back to the castle as he and the Prince wished to go somewhere on foot, and alone.

Then the two men descended to a place behind the platform, and there they put on large cloaks and great floppy hats that almost covered their faces as well as their hair. Then they slipped round the platform and in amongst the crowd.

Marion and her two companions had disappeared, and for a few minutes, John thought that he had been thwarted in his plans. Then he caught sight of them again on the outer edge of the crowd, and pushed his way through the throng in their direction.

The operation proved to be far more tricky than Prince John and the Sheriff had imagined that it would be, and even when they caught sight of the three women hurrying along a narrow street, another difficulty presented itself. A body of men in long brown robes and red cord belts seemed to be following the Prince and the Sheriff, and try as they would, the brown robed figures could not be shaken off.

When they arived in Sherwood Forest, things became a little easier for them, and they crept along amongst the undergrowth, keeping the women in sight with great difficulty. But they felt themselves to be unseen, and that was a great help to them. The men in brown robes followed the women closely, and made the Prince's plan almost impossible to put into operation.

It was only when the women began to pick berries, that Prince John began to hope for success. They were now deep in the forest, and the undergrowth was thick and lush. The men in brown robes lagged behind a little, to help with the berry picking operations, and it was at this point that the luck began to swing into the Prince's favour.

As he stumbled through the bushes, he almost fell into a pit that had been dug and then covered with tree branches, to act as a trap for wild boar. The men of Sherwood probably drove the boars along until they came to the pit, and then they crashed down into the hole unable to get out. Then the men would shoot them with their arrows, quickly and humanely.

John stared down into the pit, and a smile twisted his cruel lips.

At this moment, Marion wandered round a bush a few yards away from them, and John rose silently to his feet and crept up behind her. Suddenly he clapped one hand over her mouth whilst his other arm encircled her and dragged her backwards. She struggled like a mad woman, but the Sheriff helped John to hold her, and together they dragged her down into the boar pit where the three of them hid from view, covered by the tree branches that disguised the hole in the ground for the detriment of the hunted boar who normally used the hole.

Suddenly Marion broke free, and pulled the dagger from Prince John's belt and threw it at him, pinning him by a fleshy part of his left arm, to the ground.

John screamed with pain and anger, and Marion scrambled out of the hole and away in to the forest.

John forgot his pain as rage made his blood course faster through his veins, and he scrambled out of the hole after her, with the Sheriff at his heels.

Marion leaped through the forest with the agility of a deer, but luck was not running her way at this moment. Suddenly she caught her foot on the root of a tree and went sprawling to the ground.

Prince John caught up with her, and was about to drag her to her feet again and demand by sheer force to be told the way to the secret hideout, when she once more threatened him. This time it was with a dagger that she had pulled from a sheath that she wore fastened to her own belt.

"You little she cat," shouted Prince John, his voice high pitched with rage, "I will kill you for this."

"All right, kill me," cried Marion, springing to her feet, "let me have the Sheriff's sword, and I will fight you to the death, Prince John."

The two men roared with laughter, and the Sheriff drawing his sword, presented it to her with mock courtesy.

She received the sword and made one or two experimental strokes with it that made the Sheriff spring back to safety, but he was a fraction of a second too slow, for Marion carved a deep wound on his left cheek that was to leave a scar that he was to carry for the rest of his life. A wound that was never to have the chance to heal properly, anyway. Then the blood began to pour down his face and down his chest, soaking his clothes with a sickening bright redness. The Sheriff pulled a kerchief out of his pocket, and tried to staunch the flow with the material.

Marion gave a tinkling laugh, and then turned her attention to Prince John.

She danced before him as lightly as thistledown, but it was only her quickness and lightness that kept her out of serious trouble for the time being, but after a while, she began to tire and she was obviously no match for the superior strength and stamina of the strong man and his furious swordsmanship. She wounded him slightly a few times, and sustained one or two minor cuts herself, before beginning to weary considerably.

Then suddenly and dramatically, the fight was over, brought to a halt by the most surprising of all figures.

A great man in monk's clothing emerged from amongst the trees and cried out in a voice that echoed through the forest, "Shame on you, John, for fighting with a woman. Shame on you for such a cowardly act."

Prince John stopped fighting on the instant, to stare in amazement at the man who had dared to address him in such a manner. He stopped fighting in a flash, but not before Marion had sent his sword flying through the air, to land at the feet of Robin Hood who had just broken through the undergrowth with a band of men at his heels.

Prince John and the Sheriff looked as though they would attack the new arrivals, but John threw up his hands helplessly, when he realised that both his dagger and his sword had gone. The blood was soaking his sleeve where Marion had pinned him down with his own dagger at the bottom of the boar pit, and he began to feel a little weak from loss of blood, and also from shock.

The voice of the monk was familiar to him, too familiar, and he almost collapsed as he saw all his hopes and dreams and ambitions melting like snow flakes in the sun of a warm spring day.

"Stop this nonsense, John," cried the monk. "Get down on your knees and beg my forgiveness."

There was tense silence in the clearing, and all eyes were turned on to the face of Prince John. He had gone deathly pale, and his eyes looked stupified with shock.

"Down on your knees, I say," cried the monk, "do not argue. Down on your knees to your superior, Prince."

John sank to his knees, unable to stand on his feet any longer, and he looked up at the man who towered above him.

The monk threw off his robes, and stood revealed in his suit of black armour. Then he raised his great arms and took off his helmet, to reveal his face for the first time.

All those present sank to their knees, and Robin Hood felt the tears course down his weather-beaten cheeks as he said in a choked voice, "Richard. King Richard. Richard the Lion Heart."

Then Prince John fell forward in a dead faint.

Chapter XIX

ANOTHER ADVENTURE BEGINS

A LOG fire burned brightly in the massive hearth of the great hall at Locksley Hall, and the lord and master of the beautiful old house and its prosperous farm lands around it, gave a very deep sigh.

"What kind of a sigh was that," asked his lady, glancing up at him anxiously, "was it a sigh of contentment, a sigh of impatience, or a sigh of regret?"

Sir Robert Fitzooth smiled down at her from his great height and smiled gently. He gave her a very long and silent look of deep affection before answering her questions. He gazed in admiration on the face that did not seem to have grown an hour older during their long and adventurous life together, and his eyes travelled on to the trim figure that was now wearing flower-strewn lilac silk instead of the neat suit of Lincoln Green or the peasant woman's dress that she had graced so charmingly for so long.

The little stone house that they had built with their own hands at the secret hiding place in the heart of Sherwood Forest, was now a thing of the past. It was now occupied by a forrester and his wife, who had lost everything that they posessed to Prince John and the Sheriff of Nottingham.

Then Robin began to answer his wife's questions.

"A sigh of regret, or impatience, or satisfaction," he said quietly. "A sigh can mean so very much, can't it? Well, I dare say that my sigh was caused by a mixture of the three feelings. First of all, regret because I am no longer surrounded by all my men who served me so well and so faithfully during those long years in the forest, adventurous years that were bound to leave behind a feeling of restlessness. Impatience because I sometimes have the feeling that I want to be doing something constructive again. Satisfaction because I have achieved all that I have always wanted most, and that is a wife and a home and children, and King Richard ruling us all on his throne."

"Yes, Richard is ruling us well," replied Marion, "but I hear that he too gives a great sigh of impatience because he wishes to be on the war-path again. You men are never happy, unless you are engaged on some wild venture. Oh, Robin, why won't you realise that you and I are growing older and we have our children's welfare to consider. I do not wish them to grow up in a warlike England."

"There will always be wars," said Robin gently, "because other countries will always be jealous of this green and pleasant and happy land of ours, and wish to have it for themselves. That is the way of life ... and death. There is nothing we shall ever be able to do about it, except fight and die for our freedom. Englishmen will often have to do that, my love."

Marion sighed and her eyes filled with tears for a few moments, before she wiped her tears away and returned to the sewing on her knee.

Robin turned to place another great log on to the fire, and it was at this moment that Little John knocked lightly on the door and then opened it to put his great head into the room.

"We have a visitor, Robin," he said, a note of excitement making his voice tremble a little.

"If it is that Sheriff again," growled Robin, "kill him and throw his body to the dogs."

Little John stepped aside after opening the door to the full, and then he bowed low as the guest entered the room.

Robin and Marion sprang to attention as the visitor marched in, and then made their obeisances to King Richard who was now dressed in the clothes of a King at peace and not in his famous black armour.

The King took them both by the hand and greeted them as two old and trusted friends, and Little John then received his share of the welcome.

Wine and cakes were brought for the King's refreshment, and when he had been seated and refreshed after his ride out of Nottingham where he was visiting on business at the moment, Robin and Marion seated themselves before him and settled down to listen to what he had to say.

"I trust that you are all well and happy and at peace," said King Richard, "and that all your merry men are now settled down to their new and peaceful way of life."

"Many of them are married and have families and businesses now," said Robin, "and the older ones and their wives are prospering on the farms or businesses that were taken from them in the bad old days. But the younger unmarried ones are still restless, and anxious to be on the go again. Some of them have joined the army or the navy, but the lists of England at peace are full now, and cannot take all the men who wish to join up."

King Richard stared down at his peacetime shoes that fitted so strangely on to his soldier's feet, distastefully.

"So the men are restless, are they," he said musingly, "and so am I, sad to say. I lost my lands in Normandy, and now I feel that by rights, I should be in full possession of my properties overseas. But they are held by powerful men, and I shall have to fight hard to invade France and get my lands back again. I shall need a great many men if I am to achieve my aim, Robin. I shall need all the men that I can muster, and that is why I came to see you today. I shall need all the men that you can spare, the men of Sherwood are just what I need behind me right now. Would you consider calling them together so that I might speak to them?"

Robin smiled and rose somewhat stiffly to his feet, for the long hard years had taken their toll of him, and now the aches and pains and stiffness caused by sleeping out in the forests a few times too often, was turning him into an old man before his time.

His wounds played him up also in a painful way, and although Marion tended him to the best of her ability and the doctor prescribed treatment for him, there was nothing that anybody could do to restore Robin's lost youth and fitness.

He walked over to the great mantelshelf and picked up the lucky horn that had served him so well over the years, when his life had been in great danger, and then he walked out of the room with Richard and Marion and Little John at his heels.

He walked out on to the front door steps and raised the horn to his lips, and gave a mighty blast upon the instrument. His heart beat a little faster as he heard the summons once more, and Little John's mind went back to Sherwood Forest and the happy days that he had spent there.

A few moments later, a few figures came running towards him across the grass, and half an hour, later, all the available men of Sherwood were standing on the great lawn and amongst the trees of the wood that was part of the Locksley Estate.

King Richard smiled at them all, and they cheered him until they were hoarse. Then he raised his hand to request silence.

Like all good fighting men, he was no good at fancy words, and so he went straight into the matter on his mind. He told them of his need for good fighting men to take to France with him, and he asked those who wished to follow the flag, to report to his palace in London to sign on for duty.

Then he thanked them all for listening to him, and then returned to the great hall to warm himself at the log fire whilst Marion hurried away to supervise the cooking of a meal for him.

"What is the news of your people, Robin," asked the King, "how are they faring? Your very closest friends, amongst so many."

"Friar Tuck returned to his hermits cave at Copmanhurst," said Robin, and he has built himself a little house there, and is building a chapel to the Honour and Glory of God. He tells me that if ever I need a place of refuge again, he will give me food and shelter. But I do not suppose that I shall ever have to avail myself of his hospitality in that respect. Although Marion and I often visit him."

"We do that," put in Marion, "and then for days after we return home, Robin's heart and mind are back in Sherwood with his band of outlaws."

Robin gave a warm smile, and then went on to say, "Little John lives here with me, and seems to be happy enough although he is like me, not getting any younger or livelier. Allan-A-Dale and Lorna now live on the farm that you gave to them when we were all pardoned and given back our possessions, and they have four children and another one on the way. Allan still raises that voice of his in song, and it gets better and better as the years go on, unlike my weary old body."

"What about George-A-Green and Betriss," asked Richard, "are they well?"

"They are happy on their old farm in Wakefield," replied Robin, "as you know, Will Scarlet was killed, and now rests where I would like to rest some day, and that is in some quiet woodland glade with God's skies and trees above me, and the good Mother Earth and her country around me. With my beloved wife at my side, when the time comes."

"You have a family of children also, Robin," said the King, "how are they? I must see them before I leave you today."

"I have five children now," said Robin, "a set of twin boys, two other sons, and a daughter who is the image of her mother. They are well and happy in this peaceful England of ours, thanks be to you. Your Majesty."

During the meal that followed, Robin talked of peace-time things, but although the King listened attentively and asked many questions, his mind was a quarter on the war that lay ahead of him. Secretly, he was looking forward to it.

After the meal, he interviewed Robin's five children, and gave them a gold coin each which they treasured for the rest of their lives.

When he left the house, a large body of Robin's men were ready to follow him, bearing their bows and arrows and swords and daggers and lances and what armour they had. Their eyes were alight again at the thought of being in action again, even if many of them were to die for their King. After all, there was no better way to die.

Only thirty men remained behind, men who could not bear to be parted from Robin Hood and Marion, in spite of the fact that they might so easily be following their King into battle.

Robin watched the horsemen depart, and felt a glow of excitement stir in his heart. Then he thought to himself that after all, his own adventures might not be quite at an end.

Prince John was still very much alive, and so was the young Sheriff of Nottingham, and as long as they were alive to draw breath, Robin would always have two extremely dangerous enemies.

Prince John was backed up in every action, however black, by the Sheriff who was far more evil than his old uncle, and that was saying a very great deal.

Chapter XX
A BLACK DEED

PRINCE JOHN settled down to the business of gaining power in England quietly and furtively, hoping that at any moment, a messenger would arrive to bring him news that Richard had been killed in battle. The wars were not going well for Richard in France, and John waited hungrily in the Royal palace, pacing up and down his room for hours on end, his brows creased into a frown and his hands clasped tightly behind his back. Each time the door opened, he would spring round like a wild animal, to see who was entering the appartment, almost praying for his brother's death.

He was leaving Robin Hood severely alone for the time being, but he had not forgotten the man who had ridiculed him so unbearably at Ashby-De-La-Zouche. He was waiting for the moment when he could turn the tables on the ex-outlaw and finally and as painfully as possible, dispense with this hated enemy.

Little John often heard rumours about the wars in France, and of Richard's ill fortunes of war, and he worried unceasingly about the fate of so many of his late comrades from Sherwood Forest.

News of defeats and set-backs began to reach Little John and Robin through reliable sources, and their hearts sank as they realised that they were not listening to mere rumours set going by Prince John. The informants were men of Sherwood returning too badly injured to fight any more for their King.

One Sunday morning after a particularly distressing piece of news had been brought to Locksley Hall, Robin decided to go in to Nottingham to go to Church in order to pray for his beloved King Richard and his armies.

"Be careful, Robin," said Little John, "let me go with you. Also please take a few armed men with you. Prince John is in Nottingham, and I have a strong feeling that he is only biding his time to get the better of you. I have a strong premonition that he will try to play some trick on you today, as you leave the Church."

"I can look after myself," Robin said stubbornly, his mouth setting into determined lines, "I want you to stay here and look after Marion. If John plays a trick, it will be on her, for she too made a fool of him when she fought him in the forest, the day that Richard came back to us and proclaimed himself. Stay here, and don't let any harm come to her. I leave her in your hands, John."

Robin bade his wife farewell, and she clung to him desperately as she pleaded with him not to go in to Nottingham that day, but Robin's mind was made up. He kissed her and put her gently from him, and then hurried out of the house, leaving her weeping in Little John's arms.

"I feel that today will bring the end to all our happiness," she sobbed, "something dreadful is going to happen. I can feel it in my heart. Oh, I do wish that he had not gone."

Little John comforted her as well as he could, but he too felt that Lady Marion might be in just as much danger as Robin, and was less able to defend herself than Robin, who could deal with any enemy that dared to face up to him with great strength and endurance.

Robin rode into Nottingham alone and unarmed, to the Church where he prayed for the safety of Richard and his men, and also for their success. Then he emerged from the Holy building, to look up at the sky that had grown suddenly dark and menacing whilst he had been praying.

Suddenly the Sheriff's scribe hurried up the Church steps and said, "Sir

Robert. Can you come quickly to the castle? The King has returned and wishes to speak to you."

Robin sprang on to his horse and galloped away to the castle, with the scribe riding after him. When they reached the great building, he hurried in to the main entrance to find the Sheriff himself waiting for him anxiously.

"Follow me, Sir Robert," said the Sheriff, a note of excitement making his voice tremble a little.

He led the way up the great staircase and then up a second flight of steps, and along a corridor, to lead the way up a long spiral stairway up and up until Robin thought that they were never going to reach the top.

They moved upwards past small landings and doors, up and up and up and up. Then suddenly the steps came to an end, and they found themselves entering a small room that had only a tiny barred window for light and air.

At the far end of the room stood the figure of a man.

It was Prince John.

"Where is the King," asked Robin Hood.

Prince John gave a thin smile, and the Sheriff barked with laughter. Then Robin knew that they had trapped him at last. He heard the sound of running feet coming up the stairs, and then he felt his arms being seized and held from behind.

"Tie him to that ring in the wall," ordered Prince John, "and then begin to wall up the door. This time he shall not get away from us, ever."

The Sheriff and Prince John stood watching him, as the soldiers tied Robin to the ring, and then the two men came and looked closely into the face of the man who had outwitted them so many times, and caused them such woe. The man who had always proved himself to be so elusive, until now.

They jeered at him for a while, and then turned and left him alone, to listen to the sounds of the wall being closed up for ever, leaving him alone to die.

Before the last bricks had been put in place, Prince John called through the hole, that he would marry Lady Marion himself that same night.

Robin was so blinded with fury, that he felt no pain as he tugged and fought against his bonds. Suddenly the rope broke, and his hands were free. He hurried to the window, found that three of the bars were so rusty and broken that they could be dragged from their sockets. Then he climbed up on to the window-sill and looked out, down at the dizzy drop below, and saw that there were no hand- or foot-holds by which he could escape. The drop to the ground was a killer, he could not escape that way.

Then he remembered the silver bugle horn that he always carried in the pouch that he wore on his belt, and produced the instrument. He drew a deep breath and blew a mighty blast on the instrument, and then waited for results.

Minutes later, he heard the sound of his own horn being blown, and smiled for the first time on that black day. He pulled off his shirt and hung it out of the window, fastening it by the sleeve to one of the bars, and then he settled down to wait patiently for whatever rescue operation might be staged for his benefit.

It was quite dark by the time that help came in the form of an arrow. It shot through the window, and Robin leaped to his feet to pick it up.

A thin thread was attached to the arrow, and Robin began to pull in the thread. Yard after yard of it was pulled through the window and rolled into a ball, before the end of a strong rope came into view.

Robin tied the rope firmly to the bars, and then squeezed out through the space that he had made by removing the loose bars. Then he slowly climbed down the rope, his feet walking down the wall of the castle, until he was twenty feet above the ground.

Then disaster struck. The rope broke, and Robin crashed down on to the ground, to lie injured and unconscious.

Little John and his followers ran to Robin's side and lifted him carefully on to his horse, and tied him securely in to position. Then they moved away through the silent and empty streets and into Sherwood Forest.

They had only travelled two miles when they heard the thunder of hooves behind them, and drew hurriedly off the road to hide amongst the trees. A band of fifty heavily armed men on horseback rode past their hiding place, and in the centre of them all, was Prince John.

"Make haste," he shouted, "I must reach London before noon tomorrow. This news looks promising."

Then the horsemen rode on and out of sight, leaving Little John to realise that Prince John was to be out of harm's way for a little while. Something had happened to recall him to London suddenly, and then John began to worry as to the nature of the news.

When the horsemen were out of sight and sound, and there was no sign of any followers, Little John led his men to Friar Tuck's cave at Copmanhurst, so that Robin could rest and be cared for until it was safe for him to be out and about again.

Friar Tuck received his charge in a state of consternation, and anxiously supervised the carrying of Robin into the little house, and there they placed him on Friar Tucks own very comfortable bed, so that he could rest peacefully and recover from his hurts.

Little John stayed until Robin was conscious again, and then he returned to Locksley Hall, to give the news to Lady Marion. He was not looking forward to the task.

Robin had given him a message to pass on to Marion, and Marion listened white-faced as Little John told her not to try to visit Robin yet. It might give away the fact that he was still alive and in hiding, and if any of the Sheriff's men followed Marion to the cave, it could lead to severe complications.

As far as Prince John and the Sheriff knew, Robin was walled up in Nottingham Castle and well and thoroughly dead by now.

Robin was content to let them go on thinking on those lines.

Chapter XXI

A TERRIBLE THING

ROBIN HOOD slowly came to life again as he lay on the warm soft bed in the little house in the forest, and he opened his weary eyes with an effort, to see Friar Tuck bending anxiously over him. Then his nose caught the smell of luscious soup.

"Try to take a spoonful, Robin," said Friar Tuck gently, raising Robin's head on one powerful arm. With his free hand, he fed Robin with a spoon, and almost at once, the invalid began to feel the strength returning to his limbs. When he had taken the full bowl of delicious soup, he tried to sit up and look around him, but he gave up the attempt when he felt the violent pains shooting up his back and his neck, and also felt as though his inside had been torn loose.

"You must not try to move yet," said Tuck gently, "just give yourself time to recover from that bad fall. Even a man like you cannot fall twenty feet without suffering some injuries. You will soon be up and about again, but give it time. You will soon be as good as new."

"That is just what I do feel like," groaned Robin, "as good as new, a new-born baby with not much more strength."

For weeks, Robin lay ill and under Friar Tuck's tender care, and then he began to improve and recover from his various hurts.

He was almost fit again when a messenger brought black news for them, news that King Richard had died of his wounds in France, and was lying waiting burial at the Abbey of Fontevrault, his heart was to be buried at Rouen, the town that had been so faithful to him. The war with France was over and lost, and even worse still, John was now King of England.

"I must see him again," said Robin, his eyes filled with tears, "I must get to France somehow to look for the last time on his face, and go to his funeral."

"I will go with you, Robin," said Friar Tuck firmly, "for I do not relish the thought of you making that long journey alone. We will set forth at once."

So Robin and Friar Tuck prepared their horses and got some food and money together for the journey, and then rode the long road to Dover and on to France by boat, spreading the news of the King's death as they went.

Robin put on the time-honoured disguise of the outlaws, a brown robe and a red cord belt, and with a heavy heart he paid his last respects to Richard as he lay in state, mourned by his sorrowing friends who filed past his bier in a long and weeping procession.

After the funeral, Robin and Friar Tuck returned to Sherwood, to find yet another messenger awaiting them. As soon as they rode up to Friar Tuck's little house in the forest, one of Robin's old companions ran out of the door to tell them his news.

"Lady Marion has been forced to take sanctuary at Kirkleys Priory, as King John has ordered her to be brought to him at the palace at Westminster," said the messenger, "his eyes rounded with horror at the very thought of such a thing. The children are in the safe keeping of her father, Lord Fitzwalter."

Robin and Friar Tuck rested and fed whilst they made their plans, and then they rode off once more, this time to Kirkleys Priory where they were ushered into the building and into the presence of the Prioress.

Robin kept his hood pulled down over his face, and did not speak a word. Friar Tuck explained to the Prioress that his brother was under a vow of silence, and could not speak to anybody.

Robin and Friar Tuck knew that the Prioress had no love for Robin Hood, and so it was wisest for him not to reveal his true identity to her.

"We have come on an errand from Fitzwalter," said Friar Tuck, "and he wishes to know if his daughter, Lady Marion Fitzooth, is well and safe."

"Tell Lord Fitzwalter," said the Prioress coldly, "that his daughter is well and safe as long as she remains under my care in the Priory. No harm can befall her here. As soon as I can convince her that her husband is dead, she will take the veil and become a Nun. But she is obstinate, and will not believe that he is dead."

"She is a wealthy woman," said Friar Tuck gently, "and if you can convince her of her husband's death and she does take the veil, the Priory will then claim and receive all her wealth and her posessions, is that not so? Is that not the new law that King John has made?"

"It is indeed," said the Prioress with a smile, "she will bring in a large fortune with her to the Priory."

A hard glitter lighted up the eyes of the Prioress, and her hands clutched at each other greedily, as though she was already holding the Fitzooth treasure.

It was with great difficulty that Robin restrained himself, but he bit his lower lip and closed his eyes, fuming inwardly as he realised that yet another trick was to be played upon him by King John and his wicked followers, of whom the Prioress was very notoriously one.

Friar Tuck rose to his feet and the two men made their departure, but they went no farther away than the nearest village. They rested and fed at the local hostelry, and it was while they were eating their bread and meat that the sound of a horse's hooves was heard on the cobbles outside. They turned to survey the new arrival who was throwing his reins to a hosteler and turning to enter the inn, and they gave cries of welcome as they recognised the visitor.

It was Little John.

He stared at the two monks for a few moments, and then approached them cautiously as though he could not believe his own eyes. Then he peered under Robin's brown hood to confirm that he was speaking to the right man.

"Robin," he breathed, "how are you? Are your wounds healed?"

"I am my old self more or less," said Robin, "how are you, Little John?"

"Worried," muttered Little John, as he turned to order food to be brought to him. "Have you heard that Lady Marion is a prisoner at the Priory, and now the Prioress has thrown a guard of the King's soldiers round the building. I saw two monks leaving the place this morning, and then a messenger rode away. After a while, a body of fighting men arrived, and are now posted round the Priory. What are we going to do, Robin? We must get her out of there somehow or other. She only went there for refuge from the King, and also because the Prioress sent a message that you had escaped from Nottingham Castle and was now at the Priory."

"We will go tonight and rescue her," said Robin.

Then the three men began to make their plans, and when night had fallen and it was quite dark, there being no moon that night but only a heavy mass of rain clouds, they set out armed as in the old days with their bows and arrows and swords and daggers, in the direction of the Priory.

The windows of the Priory were darkened by the time they arrived, as all the Nuns were now in their cells for the night and sleeping, but there was one window near the top of the building that was still lit from within, and Robin gave a cry of joy as he saw his wife sitting there looking out into the darkness.

But it was a cry that was to be cut short tragically, for no sooner had he made the sound, than an arrow hissed out of a near by tree and struck him full in the chest.

Robin fell to the ground dangerously wounded.

"Prioress or no prioress," said Friar Tuck, "we shall have to get Robin inside and his wound tended, or he will die within the hour."

He tied a white kerchief to a long stick of wood and waved it above his head, and then he and Little John picked Robin up and bore him tenderly to the doors of the priory. Friar Tuck gave a thunderous knock on the great oaken door, and then the three men were admitted inside. The wounded man was carried hurriedly but carefully to the guest chamber, where he was laid on the bed and his clothing removed so that his wound could be properly tended.

"You must leave me with him," said the Prioress, "and I and some of the sisters here will tend him and help me to remove the arrow. Please wait in the next room. Believe me, we are very expert at this type of work."

Little John and Friar Tuck glanced at each other apprehensively, but there was nothing that they could do except obey the order. They withdrew to the next room and were just sitting down, when they heard a key turn in the lock.

They found that they were imprisoned in a windowless room.

The Prioress called for four of the Nuns to come and help her, and then she returned to tend the wounded man. Before she began the business of removing the arrow, she glanced at the man's face, and then had another closer look. Then she stood motionless for what seemed an age to the waiting Nuns, and they were startled when she gave a cry of unholy joy.

"It is Robin Hood," she cried, in ringing tones "my enemy has been delivered into my hands."

Then she stared down speechlessly into the waxen face of Robin Hood, as he lay there unconscious and completely at her mercy. This was a stroke of wonderfully good luck as far as she was concerned.

Gloatingly, she pulled the arrow roughly out of Robin's chest, and then turned to stare out of the window while the Nuns cleansed the wound and bandaged it up as best they could.

When they had finished their work, the Prioress ordered them to leave her alone with the man, and she sat down at his side thinking out how best to deal with this situation.

He moaned and opened his dry lips, and she gave him a sip of water. Then his head fell back again, as consciousness left him once more.

Then she opened a vein in Robin's arm to blood him, as that was one of the only known cures in those days for most illnesses. She watched the blood flow from his arm into a bowl that she placed on the bed, and then she went to sit by the window to watch and wait.

It was not until the end of the next day that she unlocked the door of the room next to the guest room, and summoned Friar Tuck and Little John to their friend's side.

"He is dying," she said coldly, a faint smile threatening to twist her lips into a grimace of hatred. Her eyes gleamed malevolently.

The two men scarcely looked at her as they hurried to Robin's bedside, and saw what she had done to their friend and leader. She had bled him to death.

"Give me the horn," whispered Robin.

Little John picked up the horn from the table where the Nuns had placed it, and placed it in Robin's hands. Robin placed the instrument to his lips and blew a shaking note upon it.

Marion was walking in the garden when she heard the sound, and suddenly she realised that Robin was inside the building and in great trouble.

She turned and ran to the guest chamber where she now knew that he would be, and lifted Robin in her arms, weeping as she did so.

"Marion," whispered Robin, weakly, "give me my bow and arrow. I will shoot an arrow, and where it falls, you must bury me."

Little John brought the bow and arrow to his friend, and placed it in his hands. With his last remaining strength, Robin fixed the arrow into the bow and shot the arrow out of the open window.

It soared away and over the wall of the Priory, to fall in the centre of a tiny glade in the wood outside.

As the arrow struck the ground, Robin gave a wonderfully happy smile and gave a deep sigh. Then he was dead.

The following morning, Little John and Friar Tuck and Marion buried him in the little glade, in the coffin that they had made for him with their own hands, and Friar Tuck read the burial service over the grave.

Then with a last word of farewell, they left Robin to his last long and peaceful sleep.

Chapter XXII

THE YEARS THAT FOLLOWED

A shaft of sunlight forced its way through the heavily leafed trees of Sherwood Forest and came to rest on a neat little stone-built house that stood besides a stream at Copmanhurst. A brightly painted new boat lay on the shores of the stream ready to transport travellers across to the opposite bank, and a tiny chapel stood there waiting for the use of those who wished to give thanks to God for some blessing or other, or to pray for help in time of trouble.

Inside the chapel on the right-hand side of the altar, were two beautifully carved stone figures, one of a lady in flowing robes, and the other of an archer standing at ease beside her. At the foot of the statues was a simple message in remembrance of Sir Robert and Lady Marion Fitzooth. In front of the memorial was a double candle-stick, bearing two lighted candles. The scent of incense filled the Holy silent place, and the sunlight fell directly on to the tiny altar with its hand carved wooden cross.

Outside in the glade, another smell of more earthly fragrance filled the air, the scent of roasting York ham.

Inside the little house, an ancient monk was basting the meat, and eyeing the dish of fresh eggs that he was to fry in a few moments, when the roast was completely ready.

The table was set for six people, as it was never quite certain how many people might arrive unexpectedly to be fed. The little house was warm with hospitality.

Friar Tuck was disturbed in his culinary meditations by the sound of horses' hooves, and he was instantly on the alert, for the habits of half a life-time were hard to overcome, and too often he had been compelled to defend himself against King John's men when the woods were thick with men in Lincoln Green, and he himself had worn a sword beneath his monks' habit.

But now the outlaws had gone, and so had King John, and now another King sat upon the throne of England. Once more the sun dared to shine without the fear of brightening up a scene of battle or of intrigue, and the people of England could relax and go about their lawful business without fear of being tricked out of their posessions, or taxed almost out of existence.

Friar Tuck relaxed again as he remembered for the thousandth time that he need fear no foe now, and that the sound of horses' hooves on the road outside only brought a traveller of some sort or other to his chapel, or to his house for a night's shelter, or to his boat for transport across the ferry.

The travellers always brought some interesting news, and Friar Tuck had to fear no longer the arrival of bad news. Everything seemed set fair for a long run of happiness and prosperity for the often troubled shores of England.

The horse drew to a halt at his door and gave a great snort, and Friar Tuck hurried to see who might be calling on him at this hour.

He stared out at the beautiful horse for a moment in great admiration, and eyed the expensive trappings and beautiful saddle that the animal wore, and then he turned his attention to the rider who was just dismounting.

The rider was a young boy, and he too wore rich clothes, and carried his handsome head proudly but without arrogance.

"Welcome, young sir," cried Friar Tuck, "let me take your horse and unsaddle it, so that he might rest and eat of this rich grass on the banks of the stream, and drink the clear fresh waters. Would you care to come inside and eat with me? I have a meal on the point of being ready."

"Thank you, good Friar," said the boy, as he helped to remove his horse's saddle and trappings. He then laid the things on the grass, and followed Friar Tuck into the little house, to stare about him in wonderment. Then he turned his eyes to the giant of a man before him, who was now lifting a great roast of ham with a fork on to a gigantic platter and placing it on the table. A few moments later, six eggs were sputtering in a pan of hot fat, and the Friar was basting them carefully.

"I left my men back there in the forest," said the boy, "they are eating their meal further upstream. But I wanted to come here to see you alone. You are Friar Tuck, are you not?"

"I am indeed," said the old man, "I am Friar Tuck, the friend of King Richard and all that he stood for, and a colleague and friend and companion of Robin Hood, of beloved memory. Also of his wonderful lady, Marion. God rest their souls."

He crossed himself and then smiled warmly at the thought of his friends, and then he turned to the young man who was standing beside him.

"Who might you be, if I may ask," he said curiously.

"Just a boy passing through the forest with some friends," said the lad casually.

"A very important boy though, I'll be bound," put in Friar Tuck, placing a piled-up plateful of food on the table for his guest, and then helping himself to another plateful of ham and eggs.

They ate hungrily and almost in silence, and when they had cleared their plates of ham and eggs, they went on to clear away a large plateful of apple pie and cream each.

Then replete to the point of being uncomfortable, the boy said with bulging eyes, "Tell me about Robin Hood. He must have been a wonderful man. I wish that I could have met him. My father never liked him, but my Uncle Richard almost worshipped him. He did so much to help my Uncle Richard when he was in grave danger."

"Undo your belt lad if you are too full," said Friar Tuck, as one man to another, "for I can then undo mine without offending my guest."

The two males undid their belt straps to aid digestion, and then Friar Tuck said, "Did you say Uncle Richard? What was your father's name? Was it by any chance John? King John?"

"Yes, my father was King John, and he could have been much kinder to people," said the young King, "I am Henry the Third, as you may have guessed by now. I wanted to come and thank you personally for all that you did for Uncle Richard. I hardly knew him, he was always away at the wars."

"Your father was a difficult man to deal with," said Friar Tuck, his face hardening for a few moments. Then he smiled again as he poured out a flagon of fresh creamy milk for the King. "The King could have dealt better with his people if he had been more understanding and not as . . . greedy."

"The Government made him sign a paper called the Magna Carta," said Henry, "so that he could no longer oppress the people and rule England in such a despotic way, "but I don't like to think of some of the things that he did. I think in the end, he was ashamed of himself, for he did try to make amends."

"He tried to make amends when it was too late," said Friar Tuck almost to himself. "After he had caused Robin to be killed, he allowed Lady Marion to return to her house and her children, and to live in peace there. Now her sons have grown up, and they are managing their father's estate very well indeed, and their farms prosper. Robin would have been a grandfather by now, if he had lived. I often see the little children playing about in the ground of the house, and they come to visit me. Wonderful little children."

"What became of Lady Marion," asked Henry.

"She lived at home until her sons were married, and the old Prioress was dead, and then Marion went to Kirkleys Priory to live and she became Prioress until she died. She died in the bed where Robin had breathed his last so many years before. We buried her beside him in the forest glade, just as they had both wished.

"Little John too, where is he now?" asked the boy, his eyes fixed on the face of Friar Tuck in wonderment.

"Little John went to Ireland after Lady Marion went to live at Kirkleys," replied Friar Tuck, "and he became famous for his feats of strength and his skill as an archer. Then he returned to England to die, and was buried at Hathersage in Derbyshire. He was a wonderful man, I have never seen a stronger man. You would have loved him, Henry, you would indeed."

The pair sat talking until the shadows grew long in the forest, and the sun was well down in the west, and then the young King rose to make his departure, his mind filled with the thought of Robin Hood and all his adventures.

"I shall come to see you many times," said Henry, "I think you are just as wonderful as Little John or Will Scarlett or Robin Hood."

Friar Tuck smiled gently at the young King, and he said, "There is one good thing about this old world of ours. No matter who you lose in death, there is always somebody else coming along to be loved. Robin's children, and now a new young King, for example."

The boy took his hand and said, "I will always remember your words, Holy Friar."

As he was turning to go, Friar Tuck seized a basketful of roast ham and fresh eggs and thrust them into the young King's hands.

"Thank you," said Henry, as he mounted his horse, "farewell for now. I will see you again soon."

So saying, young Henry rode away, bearing the burden of Friar Tuck's gift in his arms.

"I'll be back," he shouted.

Then he rode away out of sight amongst the trees.

Printed in Germany